9 ROOMS in BALLYGLUNIN

MIKE FARRAGHER

ISBN: 1985676842
ISBN-13: 978-1985676848

CONTENTS

	ACKNOWLEDGMENTS	II
	INTRODUCTION	1
1	LADY OF THE CASTLE	5
2	ROSE COMES HOME	17
3	ADNAN	37
4	THE REPORTER	51
5	ASHES TO ASHES	89
6	CONFESSIONS	105
7	DESIGNER DISASTER	125
8	A BRAVE DAD	139
9	AN OLD FLAME	155
10	THE EXECUTIVES	179
11	THE MIGHTY FALL	191
12	THE FINAL CHAPTER	195

ACKNOWLEDGMENTS

Thank you Laura Ginsberg and Brian Blatz for your eagle-eye editing, love, and friendship. Thank you, Maura Farragher, for the fantastic cover art. Thank you, Annie Farragher, for capturing your dad in the author photo. Thank you, Linda Fennessy, for the awesome book jacket. Thank you to my "Books in the Basement" writing group for your unwavering courage and support. Thank you, Mike and Eileen Farragher, for being the best parents a human being could ask for. Thank you, Barbara Farragher, for your love. I have the best life because I am loved and supported by top-shelf people every day.

INTRODUCTION

This book was inspired by a visit to my family in Ireland that I was able to squeeze in at the tail end of a business trip last year. My uncle had lost part of his home in a fire the day before I arrived, and he and his wife Mary were temporarily housed on a large farm that had been converted into a bed and breakfast (B&B for short) about a mile away when I called on them. My remarkable Aunt Mary had a full Irish breakfast waiting for me in the new kitchen, despite the fact she was probably in shock over the fact that her old kitchen was still smoldering just up the road.

The charming innkeeper came over for a cup of tea and a chat with "the Yank." When I asked her about the house and her online B&B business, she replied, "I get the most interesting characters in this place. I should write a book!"

I looked up from my cup of coffee. "Well, you better hurry up and write it before I do."

"How do you get the ideas for your stories?" is a question I often get, and I'm sure many in the writing profession are asked the same thing. Well, that's how a writer can stumble onto an idea. There I was, minding my own business, comforting my relatives, asking a few polite questions to make small talk, when the crackle and spark of a story caught fire and, in this case, intersected with a competitive streak to get there first before the innkeeper wrote her book. As my cousin collected me for the next stop on our visit, I went outside and looked around the red doors that dotted the courtyard of these premises.

What if I filled this place with characters and put stories behind each of these doors?

What if I bought a copy of a local paper like *The Tuam Herald* and grafted stories from there onto those I read on my iPad's *The New York Times* feed to create believable Irish American scenarios lifted from today's headlines?

What if I played around a bit with the true story about the reluctant billboard supermodel in that magazine I read on the plane ride home? I mean, what else am I going to do at 20,000 feet with six more hours of flight time?

When that creative spark does catch fire, I find "what" and "if," when placed together, open the floodgates for fiction to pour out of me. And so it did, fast and furious, for two months straight. There were plenty of times when I typed "what if" on the top of the blank page, and it stayed blank for a while.

There were plenty of times when I typed "what if," and I was knocked back by the words that came out of me. In those times, I could feel the hand of God guiding my hand across the keyboard. On those magical nights, minutes would turn into hours as I furiously pecked at the laptop in the comfy chair a few feet away from my bed.

Inspiration this time around came from David Bowie. Yes, his music frequently plays in the background as I write and go about my day, but it was the example he set in the last year of his life that threw down the gauntlet for me (and any artist paying attention, for that matter).

In the twelve months leading to his death, he made videos for *Blackstar*, his highest charting album that also served as a brilliant labyrinth of subtle goodbye messages to his fans. He also oversaw *Lazarus*, the first musical based on his back catalog. Cancer sapping your strength is a great reason to stay under the covers, and I can only imagine how uninspiring it might have been to be him, as he knew he was close to the end. I read many an account about how relentlessly focused he was in creating from nothing, not bothering to tell most of his collaborators about his illness for fear that it would slow his momentum.

There was no time to hang around and wait for inspiration to strike; all there was to do was to create and then create some more.

How many times did I think I had the luxury of time to put off that screenplay I was going to write someday?

How much time did I waste sitting around waiting until the candles were lit, the work emails were answered, and the kids were asleep before I could attain some mythical, ambient condition for creativity?

By creating an album, two long-form videos, and a musical in the last year of his life, David Bowie made me look at the pace of my five books in thirteen years. I suppose that output might look impressive to someone who finds writing even one book a daunting task, but for me it looked like an anemic trickle. Yes, I have an intense full-time job for a corporation, which Bowie did not, but I do my best work when I am creating in all aspects of my life, and there are plenty of times when I'm on the road binge-watching shows in my hotel room instead of creating something. I am not flogging myself here; I just know I am capable of more.

I thank David Bowie for his example; I ended last year with a new book, a short play off-Broadway, and an option deal for a script I am tinkering with.

I also want to thank my wife Barbara, my daughters Annie and Maura, and my family and friends for giving me the space to create. Writing is a lonely life that sometimes requires me to tune the rest of the world out, which means there were times when I listened more to the voices of this B&B's inhabitants than I did to my own family. Thanks for your understanding, patience, and love.

Mike Farragher
February 2018

CHAPTER 1

THE LADY OF THE CASTLE

There's no need for an alarm when your husband moves around before dawn to milk the cows, yet Fiona Burke set one anyway for 6:30, just in case. She had been up for hours, obsessively poring over her online reviews from the guests who had stayed at her new bed and breakfast the month before. A tear, rare for her, escaped the corner of her eye and slithered down her smooth cheek as she mouthed the words of one review while reading the text over her colorful reading glasses.

Fiona Burke has created a beautiful home away from home in the majestic Crumlin Manor House estate. My extended family stayed there over the weekend to attend the funeral of our dear uncle. Fiona was there for us every step of the way, whether we were plodding through the reservation process in a puddle of our own grief or marching through the motions of burying our beloved Uncle Barry. She seemed to intuitively know what to offer, be it a warm hug or a bottomless mug of hot tea. They say the Irish are globally known for their hospitality, and the lovely Burke family is the embodiment of that. She is doing the Lord's work, and we can't thank her enough for what she did for us in our darkest hour.

"Well, if that's not a sign from God to go through with this, I don't know what is," she whispered to herself as she closed the lid of her laptop. The air escaped her body before she closed her eyes and negotiated her way out of bed.

Fiona winked at herself in the mirror, shrugged her shoulders in a circular motion to keep her joints limber, and offered herself a brave smile that masked her weariness. She applied a bright red lipstick to counter the advancing paleness around her mouth, reached for a tissue, blotted the waxy residue that had formed on her teeth with one end, and then wiped her broad, angled chin with the other end. She moved her thick mane of brown hair into a tight bun and grimaced at the sight of the gray roots at the base of her scalp. She tamed the starched white collar, tucking it back within the confines of her navy pinstripe Ralph Lauren pantsuit. She remembered falling in love and buying the suit almost two years ago in Dublin, settling for a size smaller and swearing she'd lose the weight in six months to fit into it. Now, two years later, it swam on her thin frame.

Her slingback heels clacked on the wooden staircase that led to her kitchen. Muscle memory kicked in as she put the kettle on, buttered the brown bread, and scanned the morning papers her husband had brought to the dining room table.

She looked outside the window at her guilty pleasure. The buttoned-up neighbors of her church bingo club initially scoffed at the impracticality of importing a BMW convertible into this rainy patch of western Ireland, but today was made for just such an indulgence.

Fiona collapsed the roof before backing out of her circular driveway and following the narrow tongue of blacktop through her lush green quilt of fields before turning right on the main road.

The spring wind whipped her bangs as she drove on the N17 through Claregalway. The morning sun shot through the gaps in the mossy stone walls that lined the thin roads and framed the fields where cows lazily grazed around the ruins of medieval limestone castles and manor houses. High cranes dotted the green fields that were marked for modernization. As these sleek structures jutted from the picturesque hills, they overwhelmed the narrow farm roads now littered with potholes and traffic.

"I'm not going to miss this," Fiona huffed to herself as the traffic inched toward Galway.

She eased the car into the parking spot that bore her name. She considered every muscle move as she got out of the car, wincing when she turned to close the door. She darted through the lobby and into the ladies room. She fussed with her hair a bit longer than usual and applied another coat of lipstick. She smoothed out wrinkles that weren't there from her blouse in an attempt to stop the shaking of her hands.

She walked purposefully toward the office of Paddy Rabbitte, her managing partner. Fiona smiled tightly at Aoife, the frumpy administrative assistant and shameless office gossip. *The news of this meeting would probably rocket through the office by the time I reach the parking lot,* Fiona thought.

"He's expecting you," Aoife announced.

Fiona nodded politely before walking into Rabbitte's palatial office. Paddy was on the phone, smiling broadly as he motioned her to take a seat. *Listen to that silver tongue at work,* Fiona thought. *He charms the birds out of the trees with that line of talk.*

After a few more saccharine pleasantries, he concluded the call and focused his intense gaze at her.

“Thanks for meeting me, Fiona,” he began. “I’ve hired a consulting firm to punch up our branding and wanted to run the new logo by you.”

He offered a sly smile while she inhaled sharply and widened her jaw. In bright new fonts between the images of two Greek pillars were the names Rabbitte and Dunne, as usual, but with the name Burke added to the bottom.

“Well, Paddy, you’ve left me speechless…” her voice trailed. She dabbed tears of pride and accomplishment with a crisp linen handkerchief she pulled from her jacket pocket.

“I never thought I’d see the day when you were speechless,” he replied, a whiff of self-satisfaction in his voice.

“I cannot thank you enough for this, really,” she stammered.

“Nonsense,” he replied with the wave of his hand. “You are the best litigator this town has ever seen. The teaching work you’ve been doing at NUI Galway has raised the visibility of this firm beyond our wildest dreams. If anything, this is a bit overdue, but we had to get everything lined up. You know how we solicitors are!”

She rolled her head over her shoulders for a long moment before reaching into her bag. “I have a piece of paper of my own to show you,” she said, reaching across the desk. Now it was Paddy’s turn to recover from shock. “This is a joke, right?”

“I’m afraid this is not a joke, no.”

His eyes narrowed. “You’re leaving us? Really?”

She nodded. “This was not an easy decision.”

“Where are you going?”

"Home," she replied. "I'm staying home, not going anywhere else."

Paddy frowned. He walked over to the other side of the desk, sat in the chair next to hers, and clasped her hands. "Has the cancer come back?"

"You know as well as I do that by law, you cannot ask me that," she replied with a playful wink. "If you weren't planning on adding my name on the firm before, I could sue the arse off of you to get my name on there now after that question."

His frown deepened. "Ah, sure, Jaysis!"

"For all the things you've got on your mind inside of this building, one thing you don't need to do is worry about me," she announced. "Everything is going to work out perfectly for me."

Paddy leaned in. "I know I'm the owner of this firm and technically your boss, but come on, Fiona, you know we're friends first. You're the godmother of one of my kids, and I'm the godfather of one of yours. Level with me. What is the doctor saying?"

She looked in the eyes of her closest friend for a long moment. She remembered her law professor's advice to just answer the question and never show your emotions when being cross-examined, so she kept a wave of terror and heartbreak just below the neckline so that nothing showed on her face.

"Are you leading the witness?" she asked slyly. "None of us knows when the good Lord will take us, including me, and I think this move will delay that a bit for whatever time I have left."

"Doctors would also say that doing what you love is a great way to extend your life, and I know you love the law," Paddy countered.

"That's true; I do love the law," she replied wistfully. "The commuting is a killer with all of the building going up in and around Galway, and strolling into my kitchen to a cold dinner at 8 o'clock at night is starting to get as old as I am. You've said that yourself."

"Well, no matter what's going on, I still don't peg you for the type to just sit home and be satisfied with that," Paddy said, shaking his head.

"Well, that's the thing, I am not exactly going to sit at home. You know I've been plowing money into the estate over the last few years. I've slowly started to rent out the carriage houses, first to the neighbors hosting out-of-town guests and the odd Yank cousin from America. I dipped my toe into the online waters a few months ago, and now I'm sold out for the next eight months."

"So, you're an innkeeper now? Well, that sounds quaint, but I doubt you'll be able to pull down a million euros a year doing that."

"Aye, but the millions I do have are making hundreds of thousands of euros a year just on interest, never mind the worth of the land under my feet. That doesn't even touch Johnny's patent revenue. You needn't worry about me paying the electric bill."

"Well, speaking of the man of the house, what does Johnny think of this?"

"He's going to find out right after you do," she said with a smile.

Paddy stood up. "Ah, for the love of God! Are you serious?"

Fiona craned her neck to see what the reaction was behind the smoked glass. She could see that his secretary was also craning her neck, trying to hear what was going on. "Is this the way you want to broadcast it to the firm?" she hissed. "Keep your voice down!"

"You haven't consulted with Johnny?"

"You don't think the man hasn't been begging me for years to do this? He turns 65 tomorrow, and I want to surprise him with the news. I'd appreciate you keeping this under wraps until then."

"How much time are you giving us? What about your casework?"

"I will finish my work at home and make sure not one loose end remains. I should have the Connaught Creamery case settled out of court by the end of the week. You know Kathleen has been shadowing me on the other cases for months now. That wasn't by accident. It's high time you elevate her."

Paddy smoothed out the thin strips of hair from his widow's peak with both meaty palms. "I just don't know what we are going to do without you. I mean, really. I. Don't. Know."

"You built this firm without me, and it'll bury us both. You should be proud of the institution you created."

"Would you consider staying on as a consultant? Maybe working from home if we send you case files to the house once in a while?"

Fiona rolled that around in her head for a moment. "I had envisioned a bit of a cleaner break than that, but, you know what they say, one should never say never. Why don't we schedule some time next week over lunch so we can discuss the terms of my exit and what we might be able to count on each other for over the next year."

Paddy slumped in his chair. "Well, I'll say this: this isn't the way I thought this meeting was going to end."

Fiona smiled and nodded. "It was a lot for both of us to process, wasn't it? I'll see Aoife on the way out to put time on your calendar to continue talking."

Paddy nodded, stood up, and gave Fiona a long hug. "Take care of yourself," he said.

"I'm doing that the best way I know how," she whispered, her voice choked with emotion.

She walked by Aoife's desk and smiled, having no intention of putting time on Paddy's calendar or ever seeing him again, for that matter.

She pulled into the supermarket parking lot to pick up a copy of *The Tuam Times* and a few groceries. She crammed them into the tiny trunk and continued her journey toward home. She stopped for another moment to watch the children file out of the new Crumlin School for recess; she honked the horn when she saw her friend's granddaughter on the playground.

"Hi!" the girl squealed, waving her hand frantically as Fiona drove down the road. She soon found herself stuck behind an enormous truck carrying the roof of a prefab house. She slowed to a crawl and looked to her left, inspecting the granite face of the old Crumlin school, the two-room structure where she learned to read and write. She remembered her teacher counseling them to keep their lunch bags on top of their desks to prevent the field mice from coming up through the floorboards to take a nibble. She stared once again at the roof on the back of the truck.

"Those people getting that roof will never know what that life was like," she said to no one before hitting the blinker and making a left into the driveway.

"I have a full day of exercise done just walking up that feckin' hill to collect you," her walking partner, Grace, would say every morning. The house was almost a mile off the road, and the driveway was carved in some of the lushest scenery County Galway had to offer.

To her left, a cluster of plump auburn cows swished their tails as they grazed in the midmorning sun. A few feet ahead, a dark brown bull looked at the car suspiciously. A stone wall separated the bull from the fluffed sheep in the opposite field, who were pestered by the rooster pecking the ground at their feet. High trees offered cool patches of soft grass below them in which competing goats sized one another up as they chewed up the landscape.

The sight of the majestic main house never failed to take a momentary heartbeat from her. The renovated estate house was painstakingly planned to incorporate the granite left standing from an ancient church ruin. The main steeple anchored the house from the middle, joining two three-story plaster buildings into one. A cheery glass sunroom jutted from a brick knee wall off to the side. She parked her car in the horseshoe driveway in the front side of her beloved home.

She gathered her staff of two chambermaids and a house manager to review the day's workload over mugs of tea. She quickly changed into her farm clothes of fashionable rubber boots with a flower print, yoga pants, and a thick oversized sweater before walking into the center garden where the carriage houses sat behind the main residence.

These once housed the stables and the servant quarters of the main estate. There were a dozen structures that formed a square in the middle. She looked each house over, from the tops of their black slate roofs to their whitewashed faces and down to their matching red doors. When she was done, she looked up at the sky.

"Oh, Blessed Virgin Mary and Saint Homobonus, please watch over this place and guide me in this new chapter of my life. Amen." Saint Homobonus was an Italian merchant canonized and named the patron saint of businesspeople.

She heard rustling behind her and turned to find her husband Johnny carrying a dirty bucket full of rich soil for the flower gardens.

Despite their 40 years of dating and marriage, her heart still quivered at the sight of him. As he got older, the deep creases on Johnny's face seemed to intensify the effect of his pale blue eyes on her. He had the body of a gym rat without ever having to set foot on an exercise machine, the constant demand of the farm toning his muscles into a taut frame. At sixty-four, he was still able to hop over a cobblestone fence without breaking a sweat. His black curly mane of hair was just beginning to show signs of whitening.

"You're home from work early."

"Well, you better get used to me hanging around here. I have given my notice today."

He set down the bucket in his hand, wiped his hands on his hips, and cocked his head. "Is that right? What brought that on?"

"Well, we've been talking about it, and you've been on me to do it for years now. You're not happy?"

"I am, of course," he replied. "It just came out of the blue, is all."

"I suppose. But there's no time like the present: isn't that what you say all the time? I have been logging onto the website, doing more work on marketing, and it looks like the bookings on these carriage houses are at the level where I'm comfortable stepping away from the rat race in the office."

He nodded. "Right, so. 'Tis grand. What was Paddy's reaction?"

"He didn't take it well, as you'd expect."

"Oh, I can only imagine," Johnny chuckled. "I'm sure I'll get my feckin' ear bent at the pub by him next time I run into him."

"Tell him it was my idea, and there was no talking sense to me," she replied with a giggle. "Always count on a lawyer for an alibi."

"Not far from the truth," he said. "Well, as long as you're home for good, those weeds behind you in the garden aren't going to pull themselves, woman!"

CHAPTER 2

CARRIAGE HOUSE 1: ROSE COMES HOME

Rose Burke rolled down the window of the rented car and pointed toward the limestone structure in the middle of a field.

"That's where I went to school. Got my first kiss in the corner of the playground right there from Tommy Farley."

"You've been unstoppable ever since," Luis replied.

Everything he said had that bite to it, which sometimes annoyed her. Now, she let out a belly laugh. "You can walk the rest of the way," she said, tossing a middle finger to him in the back seat.

"Watch your hands," Meg said in her cockney accent, waving Rose's elbow away from her nose in the passenger's seat. Her enormous breasts were jiggling after every pothole on the bumpy roads.

"I can't believe you grew up here," Luis said. "I've never seen so many shades of green. It's like everywhere you look could be a backdrop for our spring catalog!"

Rose nodded. "Here you thought this was just a cheap ploy to finagle a trip home on the Bold Boots expense account. I told you! I was flipping through the last catalog and looking at all the fake scenery and thinking to myself that my old hood kicks the hell out of these locations. Glad you agree."

"Unbelievable," said Meg with a nod. "This place is just perfect!"

"Wait until you see the house," Rose replied with pride. "That's the cherry on the cake!"

Rose made a hard left between the two limestone columns holding open the black iron gates. The tires ran over the three steel pipes that covered the shallow ditch to keep the cows from wandering, a mechanism her quiet and brilliant father patented before quickly making the family's second million euro fortune. Rose suddenly jammed on the brakes, sending both Luis' and Meg's devices flying out of their hands.

"What in God's name?" Meg shouted. She watched Patches the ram scamper across the walkway.

"One of the hazards of living here," Rose replied with a shrug. "You can't take your eyes off the road for one moment!"

They continued up the path toward the house.

"Seriously, you grew up here?" Meg said, taking in the beauty. "It's like paradise. What would ever possess you to cram yourself into that shitty London flat when you have this waiting for you?"

"Why, the pleasure of working for you, boss, that's what brings me into the office every day!"

"Flattery will get you everywhere, luv!"

"I'm ready to throw up back here," Luis piped up from the back seat.

Rose looked in the rearview mirror and saw Luis shoving a finger down his throat in a motion to gag. "Yeh, that finger isn't the only thing you've had in your mouth to gag on, whore," Rose shot back.

Luis clutched his slim-fit patterned shirt. "An arrow through my heart!"

Rose negotiated the tight opening of the carriage house square, parking the car in front of the first carriage house. The sheep dogs were barking and circling the car as the trio of fashionistas stepped out of it and as Fiona threw open the back door of the main house.

"Ah, you're very welcome home," Fiona said, outstretching her arms as Rose fell into them. Mother and daughter hugged tightly for a moment. Once she broke the embrace, Meg approached Fiona, who smiled broadly.

"You must be Meg. I've heard so much about you, and you are so very welcome to Ireland."

"And I you," Meg said with a nod before extending her hand. "Nice meeting you, ma'am, and I must say I just love your daughter. I can see where she gets her beauty."

"Ah, stop with the flattery and the 'ma'am' stuff," Fiona replied, waving her hand. "Please, call me Fiona." She looked past Meg. "And you must be the fabulous Luis that I've been hearing so much about!"

Luis was busy straightening the wrinkles on his tight tailored pants and tweed blazer. He fussed with his oversize scarf, looking up for a brief moment before presenting his hand for her to kiss.

"The queen BFF is here and queer," he shouted, snapping his fingers. They all giggled in the square.

"May I say you also have excellent taste in boots," he continued, looking down.

"Aye, thanks for sending them over," Fiona replied, wiggling her toes inside the rubber footwear. "Mind you, they get good use here on the farm. My Johnny swears by them as well, though he takes a penknife and peels the Bold tag off the back heel. He doesn't want the lads in the pub thinking he got all fashionable!"

"Speaking of the man himself, where's Dad?" Rose asked.

Fiona motioned over to the barn. "Where else? It's calving season. You won't see hide nor hair of him for the next three weeks. Let's get the dinner going. That's sure to bring the likes of him in!"

Luis stayed behind for a moment, fumbling with his iPhone, and began snapping pictures of the landscape.

"He does that a lot," Rose said to her mother, motioning her head in Luis's direction. "He thinks every landscape is cinematic."

"Hard to argue with him in this instance," Meg said. "Fiona, this is simply one of the most gorgeous places I have ever seen. We would love to use this landscape for our next Bold Boots catalog!"

"You're welcome to photo everything on the property, luv." Fiona replied proudly.

"Including him?" Luis asked.

They all turned around to see Johnny walking toward them, his ropey muscles covered in mud.

"Don't even come near these clean people until you've shed those clothes and showered up," exclaimed Fiona. "The state of you!"

Johnny waved. "Howya? I'll be over to see you in a minute. I'm full of muck. Let me just wash up a bit."

"You need help?" Luis purred under his breath but it was just loud enough for Meg to hear, and she nudged him in the ribs.

"Oh my God, the house looks nicer than anything outside!" Luis squealed. It was almost too much to take in. Heavy velvet drapes in deep wine colors with gold trim stood guard at each side of the windows. Muted Oriental rugs covered dark stained hardwood floors. A casual oversize beige leather couch and a big screen television were the only modern inputs in a décor faithful to its 1864 roots.

"Fiona, this is just stunning!" Meg squealed.

"This room has been featured in two design magazines," Rose boasted.

"Ma has excellent taste in everything and pays half nothing for it!"

Fiona blushed as she surveyed the antique pieces she had lovingly curated over the years. "Look at me, just standing around. You must be starving. I have tea and sandwiches all ready for you."

They were almost done before Johnny came in again. Rose stood up and toddled over to give him a hug.

Johnny embraced her tentatively, clearly uncomfortable with public displays of affection. "You're looking mighty, pet," he whispered in her ear.

"Dad, this is Meg and Luis. I work with them."

Meg struggled to stand. She waddled over to him, her large thighs making a swishing sound underneath her dress as she walked. "You have the most beautiful home. We are so grateful that you're sharing it with us."

Johnny lowered his gaze. "Ah, sure you're very welcome here any time. Fiona will make sure you want for nothing while you're here, you can see to that."

Luis extended his hand. "This CANNOT be your father," he said, looking at Rose as he shook Johnny's hand. "Older brother, maybe. Father? Never!"

Luis cocked his head to the side, nodding intently at everything Johnny said during lunch. He peppered him with questions about the farm, the livestock, and what time he had to get up to milk the cows in the morning. He clapped his hands and shouted "love it" every 90 seconds.

"You seem to have a real interest in farming, and I have some calving to do—would you like to come? I could use a spare set of hands," Johnny said.

Luis bolted out of his chair. "Sounds like fun!"

Johnny looked down. "Well, all of ye have the right boots for work on the farm. Too bad none of these shoes will see a day of hard work."

Rose shook her head. "Here comes the speech about how we're charging an arm and a leg for nothing more than a pair of feckin' wellies."

"Hold on, Mr. Green Jeans," Meg said, grabbing Luis's arm. "You have trouble walking past a butcher's case without getting queasy. You sure this is a good idea?"

"My parents ran a farm in Spain," he hissed.

"Wasn't that a fruit stand in the middle of the city?" Rose asked.

"And now, the fruit stands!" Meg howled through fits of laughter.

"Whatever," Luis said. "I don't want to keep the man waiting. Ta-ta!"

"I'm going to head over to the cabin and unpack some of my clothes," Meg said. "Thanks for a great lunch!"

Rose and Fiona watched her move slowly across the square. Rose wandered over to the mantelpiece over the fireplace and held a picture in her hands. She smiled as she stared at shot of the ginger haired man holding her in a bear hug.

"Have you heard from Colin lately?" Rose asked. Colin was her adopted brother from Croatia who looked so Irish that everyone assumed they were blood relatives.

"He's become quite the tester lately," Fiona replied with a dry chuckle. "Between finding work in the States, settling in, and now planning a wedding, he's been pretty scarce ever since he left."

"We buzz each other on social media every now and then. He seems happy."

"That's all that matters," Fiona said with a nod. Her voice trailed, and the women descended into another patch of awkward silence.

Fiona sighed. "That Meg is a gorgeous girl, really. Pity she has so much weight on her."

"That didn't take long," Rose shot back. "Why does everything come down to looks with you?"

Fiona chose to ignore the outburst. "Mind you, you've been keeping the weight off, fair play to yeh."

"And you are wasting away, Ma. Everything good?"

"This new business of running a B&B has me worn out," she sighed. "Now I'm the one who needs a good bed and breakfast!"

Rose stretched. "I need one, too. Thanks for the meal, Ma. I'm going to rest upstairs. Hope Luis is holding his own with Dad out there."

Johnny was starting to get uncomfortable and annoyed by the constant barrage of questions. "How did you learn how to farm?" was the straw that broke the camel's back. He was just about to toss off a sarcastic comment when they turned a corner and saw a cow in distress.

"Oh Jesus, she's calving early!" he said, scrambling out of his blazer.

"Oh, fun!" Luis said with a hand clap. "We get to watch the vet deliver a baby!"

"Well, you're looking at the vet and the vet assistant. Come on!"

Luis grimaced. "This is a Prada blazer, sir. I am not going anywhere near a cow in Prada."

"You should have thought of that before you offered to walk around a farm. Now, let's go!"

Johnny approached the cow. With a loud pop and a splash, the placenta pushed out and exploded everywhere, followed by two slimy hooves poking through. The air rushed out of Luis's lungs at the sight of it. He lost his legs and toppled into a loose stone wall that collapsed like a spill of heavy marbles when he leaned against it. He shrieked as he attempted to regain his footing on the mossy bed of rocks.

"Ah, sure Jayyyyysis," Johnny bellowed, looking over his shoulder at the mess that was Luis as the animal writhed in pain next to him. "You've got to be tough on a farm. You can't just waltz in with a designer boot and think you're going to hold up."

Johnny knew better than to keep his eye off the task at hand, but the cow fell toward him, and Johnny rolled out of the way, his foot twisting under the weight. Pain shot up his leg as he staggered up to guide the calf out of his mother. The torso was wriggling out of its mother when Johnny gave it a hard tug. He ground his teeth and growled with the pain as he tugged again.

Luis had gotten to his feet and crouched behind him. “Johnny, omigod, are you okay?” he asked. He made the mistake of looking over his shoulder at the sight of the calf, bloodied and covered with mucous, and that was the last thing he remembered before passing out on top of Johnny.

Johnny blacked out for a moment with the intense pain, just as Rose entered the barn. She screamed for help before rushing in to kick Luis awake and to drag her father away from the cow, who was beginning to stagger to her feet as the calf spasmed in the corner.

The next morning found Johnny in a foul mood.

“I don’t know who the bigger feckin’ eejit is: me for turning my back on a wild animal or that Luis fella raising his hand to help with no stomach for farming.”

Fiona stopped dressing his foot in ice compresses and bandages long enough to swat him gently on the knee. “Stop with that talk,” she scolded. “He was just trying to take interest in what we do here on the farm. He didn’t mean a bit of harm. He's down at the kitchen table now, and he's just in bits about what happened."

"I'll be glad to see the back of the likes of him when he leaves us; I can tell you that."

Downstairs, Luis and Meg were hatching other plans. They were whispering as Rose came in and paused when she sat down.

"What are you two scheming about?" she asked cautiously. "I know when you're up to something."

Meg cleared her throat. "I know you brought us here to look at this landscape for our next catalog, and I must admit, we were suspicious of it. But you were right on the money. We didn't expect to love it so much."

Rose took a bow. "Why thank you!"

Luis looked at Meg momentarily for approval before speaking.

She nodded.

"What we also didn't expect out of this trip was to find the centerpiece of our next campaign. Your dad is the next face of Bold Boots," he said.

Rose let out a throaty laugh. "Oh, that's a good one."

"We're serious," Meg said, her gaze tightening. "We've been saying back in the office for how long now that we have to move past the fickle teens that will drop us once the brand goes out of style and start building a new audience."

"My dad is your new audience?" Rose asked in disbelief. "Didn't you hear my mom? He peels the Bold brand off the back of the boot with a pen knife before wearing them to the pub."

"That's not the point," Luis said. "He is just the embodiment of a man's man. The muscles, the tan, the rugged complexion toasted by the Irish sun." His voice trailed off.

Rose lifted her palm to stop the conversation. "OK, I am completely freaked out right now that you have a crush on my dad."

"Be that as it may, Luis is spot-on," said Meg. "Your dad is perfect for the campaign. We were up all last night putting it together, and we'll need you to set up a conversation with him."

"He'll never in a million years go for that."

Meg crossed her arms over her ample chest. "Well, this is when the friend hat comes off and the boss hat comes on. I don't really care how you get it done, but you will get it done. There's a lot of money to be had…"

Rose cut her off, spreading her arms to a full wingspan. "Look at this place! You think money matters anything to them? They're rotten in it!"

Meg's eyes were steely. "I am looking at this place. You should take a good look at it, too. You might end up back here if you don't get this deal done." She grabbed Luis's arm as she stood up.

"We'll leave you alone for a family meeting. We're leaving tomorrow so let's pave the way for a conversation later tonight. Good luck!"

Rose stared at their backs through the window for a long moment as the pair crossed the carriage square. When they entered the carriage house, she looked up the dark stairwell that led to her parents' bedroom.

"Ah, for the love of God," was Johnny's reply as Rose unfurled the story at the foot of his bed.

"Are they serious?" Fiona asked in disbelief. "That's just wonderful."

Johnny's head turned to his wife. "Now are YOU serious?!"

Fiona closed her eyes and shook her head slightly back and forth. "Think about it for a moment."

He cut her off. "You can stack a million moments on top of one another, and the answer is still no!"

"Think about it for a moment," she said firmly, dragging out her words for emphasis. "First, it's very flattering, isn't it? I always thought you were model material, ever since the first time I laid eyes on you."

He tightened his jaw. "I know what you're trying to do. I didn't just fall off the hay truck yesterday. For the love of God."

"Hear her out," Rose pleaded.

Her mother winked at Rose before turning her attention to Johnny. "We talked about phasing in some renovations on this place and hiring more staff that we will need as we take on all these guests. We can now get to them sooner."

He turned his gaze toward Rose. "Your mother is a touch forgetful. She doesn't remember how many fields we have out back doing feck all out there and how many realtors that knock on our door week in and week out asking to take the land off us."

Rose stood up. "I need for this to happen, Da. Meg is not the type of person you say no to and expect to have a job in the morning."

Johnny's face reddened. "Did she threaten you? Because if so, that bitch can pack her bags and the quare Spanish fella she brought with her right now."

"Not exactly."

"She either did or she didn't, which one was it?"

Fiona stepped in. "Rose, why don't you leave us alone for the night, okay? We'll have this all sorted in the morning."

Rose bowed her head out of respect before walking out the door.

Fiona looked over her glasses and coughed slightly. “You’ll to get a good night’s sleep for the chores in the morning.”

Rose stopped in her tracks. “Chores?”

“This poor old fella has got a bum leg now because your friend put himself in a place he clearly didn’t belong,” she replied crisply. “’Tis the least you can do to give your poor father a break!”

Luis fastidiously separated the muck from the bottom of his boots with an old toothbrush in the courtyard as Fiona opened the door.

“Breakfast is almost ready,” Fiona said. “Grab the others and meet me in the kitchen.”

They all lined in to find Fiona, her arms crossed at the head of the table. There was a legal pad of paper with scribbles on her left as a mug of tea steamed on her right. She motioned to the table. “Have a seat and get your breakfast together. We have some negotiating to do.”

Rose’s eyes lit up with alarm. Her mother winked knowingly.

“So, if we do this, how long do you see the shoot lasting?” Fiona asked.

Meg shrugged her shoulders and looked at Luis. “I suppose five days. Does that sound right?”

Luis nodded.

"Right," Fiona continued. "I called one of my friends in a London agency. The best print models get £8,000 per day, and I believe my husband is the best. That amounts to a £40,000 flat rate, whether you use the whole week or not. We will also close off all ten rooms for yourselves and the crew for the week at a cost of £10,000."

Meg gasped.

Fiona looked over her glasses.

"Do you have something to say, dear? Spit it out."

"So, we're negotiating now, are we? Any other demands before I drive around the corner and find another farm?"

Fiona bowed her head, stifling a smile. "Well, since you asked," Fiona continued. "Now we have to talk about an agency fee."

"There was no agency involved," replied Meg.

Fiona motioned in Rose's direction. "You wouldn't have found it without her. The male model has requested that his agent gets 100 percent of the proceeds, tax free."

Rose stood up. "Oh, my God."

"That's handy," Luis whispered under his breath.

"That one is non-negotiable. The only way he would even consider it is if all the benefit went to the new Vice President of Marketing for Bold Boots."

Now it was Luis's turn to jump out of his chair. "Hey, that's not fair! I'm here two years longer than she is! I've never gotten any opportunity to advance yet."

Fiona arched her eyebrow. "Luv, it's like my mother always said: 'if opportunity doesn't knock, build a door.'"

"Eh?" Meg leaned in. "Any other demands?"

Fiona grimaced exaggeratedly as she raised her hands and pinched her fingers together. "Just one more thing. Johnny refuses to pose for a picture, you see. You can click to your heart's content as he's doing his work on the farm, but he's not going to pose for any still photography."

Luis raised his hand like a schoolboy. "Um, excuse me. I can live with that. In fact, that's along the lines of the vision I had anyway."

"Can I speak now?" Meg asked in a saccharine tone.

Fiona looked over her bifocals. "Be my guest."

"I meant everything I said about your house and this location. It's like a postcard. Really. Then again, I can go to the edge of either side of the driveway and persuade any farmer to the right or left of you to use their land for a fraction of the price."

"That might be true, but they're not going to throw in a model as handsome as my Johnny."

"I can have a dozen character models of all shapes and sizes flown here in the morning."

"You could, I suppose," Fiona answered flatly. "Might take you longer than that to get the local council to approve a film crew setting up shop. It sure helps to have relationships with those people; it can take months to get things done in this part of Ireland. I called in a favor and can get the clearance this week. You know what they say about time and money."

"Cut the crap, boss," Luis reacted with a hint of desperation in his voice. "This place is perfect, and you know it. When you factor in the fact that it is a cheap flight over here and we can stay in the rooms, it will be a lot cheaper than shooting the catalog in Australia."

Meg shot him a look that could wither a house plant. "Remind me to send you to a negotiating class someday."

Fiona grinned broadly, pulled out a manila envelope that was tucked under the legal pad, slid it across the table, and extended her hand. "Then it looks like we have us a deal. Everything we just discussed is in contract form inside that envelope. You're welcome to come anytime between now and June. That's when our first summer bookings start."

Meg and Luis got up, groggy as if they were just punched, which, in effect, they were. They shook their heads and hissed whispers as they walked out the door.

Rose sat, open-mouthed at the table. She started to cry. "Mom, I don't know what to say. You and Dad."

Fiona grabbed her daughter's hands and looked her in the eyes. "You left this house five years ago and haven't asked us for a dime ever since. We are so very proud of you and everything you've done for yourself. It can't be easy paying those rents in downtown London, and you're just like your mother: you don't ask anyone for help. So..."

Rose wrapped her arms around her mother's shoulders. "Thanks, Ma. Let me go up and thank Dad."

Fiona nodded. "Yes, but there will be a time and place for that. I have to break the news to him first."

Rose's jaw slackened. "Wait. Dad doesn't know about this?"

"He does, and he doesn't," Fiona said with a sing-song response. "I heard him all night saying, 'well, IF I were to do it, I would want this for Rose,' and so on. So, I took all the demands he had and wrote them all down on the legal pad. I'll tell him what I agreed to, and if he gives me any guff, I'll tell him I was just following orders."

It was the first time both women had laughed together in years. It made Johnny hobble down the stairs. "What's so funny?"

Fiona turned to Rose. "Did I mention that Luis is going to have to hide the camera in the bushes as he takes the pictures?"

The women exploded in giggles.

"Are you sure you know where you're going?" Johnny asked, the nervousness welling up in his voice as they walked the narrow cobblestone alleys of central London. This was the first time he was in a city bigger than Galway, and certainly the first time he had been on a plane. The whole experience was beginning to make him jittery.

Rose locked elbows with him and held his hand for support. "We're almost there. I promise it'll be worth it!"

Rose turned her head and frowned at the sight of her parents. They appeared small and brittle in this alley, unsure of their footing both physically and mentally as they moved through this unfamiliar city. They were suddenly hit with a wall of sound from an urban bustle that had reached fever pitch as they turned the corner on the Trafalgar Square. Below the jumbo video screens that lit the night sky with bright flashes of advertisements were pushy foreign men in aprons selling discount tickets for tours and theater tickets. The hum of activity added to the suspense of the big reveal, and any thoughts of frailty were lifted at the sight of the gargantuan black and white image on the billboard in the middle of the action.

Johnny was there, blown up to 40 feet, the braided musculature of his biceps peeking out of his short-sleeved shirt as he tossed a bale of hay over his shoulder with a pitchfork. The Bold logo peeked out just under his tweed pants, which were held up by thick suspenders that only accentuated his athletic frame. Underneath him, in block letters, was a quote. "You can't just waltz in with a designer boot and think you're going to run a farm." —Johnny Burke, County Galway, Ireland.

Fiona squeaked with glee. "Oh, my God. It is just brilliant. I just can't believe it."

Johnny, a man of few words, had even less to say. "Ah, sure Jayyysisss."

Rose gently nudged him. "Better get used to it now, Da," she said with a giggle. "You're a right fashion model now."

"I'm gonna have to beat the women off with a stick," chimed in Fiona. "I have never felt more proud of you, Rose. It just looks gorgeous. Fair play to you, masterminding an entire UK advertising campaign like that."

Johnny looked at Rose. "UK? This is all over the UK?"

Rose nodded. "This is the first billboard that has gone up," she replied, unable to hide her emotion. "Billboards just like this one are going up in Wales, Scotland, and Dublin for the initial rollout."

Johnny's mouth remained open. He steadied himself against a lamp post, just a few feet from the whizzing traffic. "Can you imagine?" was all he was able to get out.

Fiona threw her arms around him. She rested her head on the shoulder of his green tweed jacket. "All these years, you stood outside of the spotlight as we got our promotions and won our awards. Now, the spotlight is yours, my love. No one is more deserving of this than you."

"I never wanted this," he whispered.

She leaned into him. "Well, you've got it now whether you want it or not," she replied. Fiona broke their embrace, lifted her hands in the air, and exclaimed in full throat: "I've always wanted to sleep with a male model, and now I'll get my chance tonight!"

CHAPTER 3

CARRIAGE HOUSE 2: ADNAN

With a hard push of the stick shift with the ball of her hand, Grace jerked the car to a stop in front of the lacquered red door of the second carriage house. She looked in the mirror, adjusted her horn-rimmed glasses, ensnared her hair in a kerchief before tying it around her neck, opened the creaky door of her car, and leaned into the cold rain. Her recent hip replacement made her wobble slightly as she walked toward the door. She craned her neck to look in the window as she furiously knocked on it. A long dark figure leapt from his chair and opened the door.

"Howya, Adnan?" Grace said, fussing with the kerchief as the rain pelted her. "Just wanted to let you know I'm here, and I'll come to collect you in a few minutes. I'm just going to have a quick cuppa tay with Fiona in the main house."

Adnan shrugged his shoulders and smiled weakly.

"Right. I forget you have no idea what I'm saying."

She hobbled across the courtyard and rang the doorbell of the main house. There was a weak "come in" that could be heard through the door, and she opened it. She closed her eyes and took in the smell of a roaring turf fire and fresh-baked scones that greeted her as she walked into the kitchen.

"Jaysis, it smells brilliant in here," Grace said to Fiona, whose back was to her at the sink.

"Howya, Grace, I'll be with yeh in a minute," came the reply. "Johnny and I pulled the most gorgeous rhubarb in the garden this morning, and Maya's just rolled the dough out for a pie. Bridie is in the next room, and the kettle is warm on the stove. If you don't mind fixing the tea on your own, my hands are a little..."

Grace cut her off. "Not a bother at all. I just checked in on our Syrian friend, and he's getting himself together. I'm dying for a cup after that lashing rain out there."

"'Tis a feckin' ark we'll need, not a car, if this rain doesn't let up. Does Adnan know you're here?"

"Yah, he does," Grace said as she wrapped the tea towel around the handle of the kettle and poured the tea into the mug. "I'll run him over to O'Malley's in a little bit. Has he been a bother to you?"

"Och, sure not at all," Fiona said dismissively. "He's as polite as can be. Maya's become an expert at making the scones. The kids are dotes. They can't get enough of the horses and cows outside, and we have them pulling the weeds and spuds from the garden. It's so cute to watch the wonder in their faces."

Grace bit the inside of her cheek. "No rudeness or anything like that?"

Fiona made eye contact through the mirror in front of the sink. "No. Should there be?"

"Well, there is a little edge to yer man once in a while all right," Grace replied.

"How so?" Fiona inquired.

Grace looked out the window before speaking. "As an example, he almost tore the head off me the other day, or at least it seemed he did, what with the broken English and all."

"What brought that on?"

Grace cleared her throat. "Well, I merely mentioned that there were about a million other things the family needed besides that new iPhone."

Fiona turned around and put her hands to her hips. "Jaysis, Grace, what do you expect?"

Bridie came into the room and nodded briefly at Grace. At 87, Bridie was almost old enough to be the mother of the other women in the room but looked just as young. A Miss Galway of 1955, it seemed that the ravages of eleven children or age had no effect on her soft skin and feline movements.

"People talk, is all," Bridie said meekly, pressing the delicate china cup to her pursed lips. "You raise all this money for our adopted Syrian family, bake sales and everything else for the poor creatures, and then he's walking down the street with a phone nicer than most of the people in the parish..." Bridie paused and grimaced for dramatic effect.

"Exactly," Grace said, winking as she pointed her finger in Bridie's direction. "We all work very hard for our money, and there's plenty of us who'd like the latest cell phone."

This made Fiona cackle. "Sure, you're rotten in money, Grace, who are ye foolin'? Besides, you could barely manage your way around that ten-year-old flip phone with the cracked screen!"

"You know what I mean," Grace said, waving her off. "Makes you think twice about being charitable, I can tell you that."

"If you want to be perfect, go sell your possessions and sell to the poor, and you will have treasures in heaven. Then, come follow me," Fiona said firmly. "I believe that is the Gospel of Matthew 19...verse 20, or is it 21?"

Bridie shook her head and smiled. "Och, sure Grace, that's what we get for electing a lawyer to head our Bible study group. There's no winning with her. Quit while you're ahead!"

Grace was quick to change the subject. "I'll drop Adnan off at work, then I'll come back and get ye for a walk. Sound good?"

Fiona grimaced. "Ah, sure, I'm not able for it today. I think I'm coming down with something, and I want to save my energy for the weekend. The cabins are fully booked!"

Bridie furrowed her brow. "That's the third time this week you've bowed out because you're not able. Everything all right with you?"

Fiona nodded and spoke evenly. "I'm fine."

"Well, we all agreed to walk every day to keep off the pounds, and I don't want to lose the momentum we have," Bridie replied. "Not that you seem to need it Fiona. You're wasting away."

"That must be the new clothes," Fiona replied with a flat chuckle. "There's still plenty of fat if you look up close."

Adnan bent the vinyl blinds and looked at the women through the window in the main house. He squinted as he ran his spidery fingers through his long and tight black beard. Among his many worries, he was now concerned that the patience and generosity of these Brooklodge Church ladies was wearing thin; he didn't always catch what Grace was saying underneath those steamed whispers and the thick, rapid-fire accent, but he could sense the sharpness in her tone when they interacted lately. The thick Irish brogue was thick and in sharp contrast to the melodic tones of the British professor that taught them English, which made the language barrier worse sometimes.

He looked in the mirror, pawing at the dark circles forming under his eyes. The nights of fitful sleep were taking their toll; the slamming of a barn door conjured up memories of gunfire, and the ancient ruins in the fields around Tuam reminded him of the crumbling streets of his beloved Aleppo. All of this refueled his unrelenting night terrors.

The case worker assigned to him had suggested he meditate to quiet his mind after what she described to Adnan as "a trauma." She had him download an app on his phone that guided the meditation. He put a towel on the floor, sat cross-legged on it, clicked the app, and closed his eyes.

Stars and light bursts danced on the inside of his eyelids as his mind settled. As the phone emitted gentle cricket and waterfall sounds, Adnan's mind went to a drier place: the desert of his beloved Syria. The wind had made stepped layers of auburn sand across the landscape, and Adnan concentrated on the soft shifting of the grains as the wind blew. He could feel his body slacken.

A large bird circled around the sun overhead, casting a shadow on the sand with its wingspan and made him tense again. Adnan squinted harder to remove the bird from his meditation, but the bird guided him toward the rubble. The dark bird appeared motionless in the bright sky, riding the shifting breezes in a circular motion before landing in a pile of concrete.

"No," Adnan whispered. Shaking his head.

Adnan could see the vulture's black eyes scan the jagged concrete, hopping across pulverized stone toward the bottom of the heap. The vulture craned his neck through a space in the concrete, shaking its head violently as it tore the flesh from the finger of a dead body crushed underneath.

Adnan's eyes flung open in panic as he wiped the dewy sweat off his brow with his sleeve. The case worker encouraged him to keep at the meditation, but it always ended the same way.

He walked to the other side of the room, grabbed the apron that was draped over the chair, and stuffed it into his knapsack. He glanced over to the other side of the room at the crooked 8-by-10 framed piece of paper that housed his degree, the only proof he had of the medical miracles he routinely made as Head of ER at Damascus Medical Center.

He hopped over the large puddles that seeped through the gravel in the driveway on his way to the main house. He strode through the kitchen where his wife, Maya, was speckled with flour as the newly hired head cook attempted to show her how to make Irish scones. She had abandoned the long tunic of their homeland as soon as she arrived in Ireland, favoring the form-fitting fashions of the locals, and Adnan seemed to be in an almost constant state of arousal at the sight of her.

"Smells good in here," he said in their Arabic. "Can I have one before I head off to my ever-so-challenging work as a dishwasher?"

Maya offered a weak smile and raised her bushy eyebrows underneath the white habib that covered her hair. She motioned her head in the direction of the other room.

"Did I see Grace wearing a habib, or was it just the rain?" Adnan giggled, and soon she joined him.

"You always know when to say the right thing at the right time," he said, lifting the back of her headdress and kissing the back of her neck from behind.

"I know this work is beneath you, but it's not forever," she whispered in his ear before kissing it. "It will get better. I love you for everything you're doing for us."

Grace entered the room. "Are you ready, pet?"

Adnan nodded slightly.

Grace smiled at Maya. "Right, so. I'll take this one out of your hair so you can get cracking on the baking. You're doing marvelous. The place smells fantastic!"

Maya smiled and bent her head bashfully. "Thank you," she replied in halted English.

Grace said nothing during the three-mile ride to O'Malley's, an oversized structure that housed a bar and a restaurant connected to a funeral parlor.

"I'll come to collect you at 10," she said as he eased out of the car.

"Thank you," he replied in broken English. "I call you."

"Very good," she exclaimed in elongated baby speak, which infuriated him. He might not have known everything she was saying, but the tone said it all.

The car pulled up in front of O'Malley's, a pair of matching houses connected by an enclosed walkway. One O'Malley brother owned the bar while the other owned and managed the funeral parlor next door to it. "We'll get them coming or going," their father exclaimed to the press the day he broke ground on the compound.

Adnan's lanky frame stretched out of Grace's car like a praying mantis caught in mid-yawn. He straightened his shoulders as he slung the knapsack over his back and walked through the door.

A tired log of fluorescent light flickered on the ceiling as Timmy O'Malley, the bar owner, washed pint glasses behind the bar. He nodded cheerfully, and Adnan waved before cramming himself into the small shed in the backyard to haul kegs of Guinness—that's the dark beer everyone seemed to order nonstop that began with the letter "G"—over to the back of the bar. Adnan shimmied a keg onto a wheelbarrow and pushed it toward the bar.

The brakes of a large tour bus hissed in the parking lot, giving the bar staff little warning of the onslaught of new customers. Within a few minutes, the tiny room looked like a swarm of bees, with the yellow and black jerseys on the Kilkenny footballers vying for a stool in search of the next pint.

One of them nudged his teammate on the shoulder, pointed in Adnan's direction, and winked. "Ah, sure Jaysis, ye'd think ye're in Dublin with all the bin Ladens walking around in this place," he said loudly to no one in particular, his words slurring under the tidal wave of liquor. "Sure, you'd be wondering now what was in those kegs he was carrying. Is it explosives?"

Timmy peered over his reading glasses, his grey eyes locking onto those of the soccer player as he spoke. "Enough of that talk. Judging from the jerseys you're wearing, I can tell you're not from around here, and I can tell you that we don't tolerate that kind of talk here in this bar."

"Do you not?"

"I do not," Timmy replied, his voice dropping to low rumble. "Adnan is over here from Syria. His home and five blocks around it were destroyed and our church has adopted him and his lovely little family. He's one of us now, and if that is something that doesn't sit well with you, take your business somewhere else."

The Kilkenny man stood up from his bar stool. "That's the problem with this country now—you actually believe he's one of us! Why the hell isn't an Irish kid doing that job? Is that the only kind you can find with all these able-bodied young boys in this county?"

"All of our jobs are being outsourced to these damned foreigners," his wobbly friend offered. "They all came over here when times were good, swooped in, took our jobs, and then fecked off back home when the money went dry. We'll be paying that damned EU bill for years, and this camel shagger will be back home buying shoe bombs with the money he made over here."

"Two things we don't tolerate in this bar is racism..."

"And feckers who sound like Trump," shouted Padraig Frayley, an enormous farmer in the corner table. "Wake up, boyo! Working in a bar is beneath these young lads nowadays. This crowd wants things to go back to the way they were, but that's not going to happen. The world has changed. Where have yeh been?"

The largest soccer fan wrapped his pale arm around the shoulders of his smaller friend and sniffed the air. "Do you smell a shite in that corner behind us?"

"Anything worse than a smell of shite is the sound of a shite mouthing off when no one fucking asked him." Padraig threw the table into the wall, creating a space next to the barstools. For a large man, he was up on his feet quickly and grabbed the Kilkenny shirts with his meaty hands.

"It's off to take out the trash is where I'm going," Padraig said with a grunt before slamming both soccer fans against the wall. His face was bright red as he stepped toward them. "You don't like the smell and sound of this place, yeh can head back on the bus that brought yeh and yer shite team up here!"

"That's enough," O'Malley said from behind the bar.

One Kilkenny fan shoved Padraig while the other grabbed a bottle of Guinness and broke it against the bar. As he raised his hand, Padraig shoved one man into the other, and the bottle opened a huge gash on the man's neck.

Tim scurried around the bar. "Ah, sure Jaysis, Padraig, look what yer after doing!"

The soccer fan put a fist to his neck as the blood poured through his fingers. Padriag recoiled in shock. The sight of his doused jersey made the man light headed, and he collapsed into a heap by the door.

"Call a doctor!" shouted one of the horrified women at the bar.

Adnan bolted from behind the bar, tearing a bar towel in half as he ran. He pried the man's hands from the wound and replaced them with long bar towel strips around his neck. He applied pressure to stem the bleeding as the man struggled.

"Get the fuck offa me!" he gurgled.

"Ice!" Adnan shouted. "I need ice wrapped in a towel!"

Tim scooped ice from the trough and ran toward Adnan.

Adnan motioned over to the funeral parlor next door. "Do you keep thread or stitches over there in the morgue?"

Tim was on his feet. "I have that and some glue we use on the eyelids. I'll bring that as well."

Adnan moved his knees up to pin the man beneath him.

"The more you move, the more you bleed," he hissed in slow, deliberate English. "You may hate me, but I will not let you die."

The bleeding man's hateful gaze soon melted into one of terror, and he stopped squirming beneath Adnan, who had called for a bottle of whiskey. Adnan doused his hands and began removing shards of glass from the man's neck. With each pluck, the man underneath him grimaced. Tim soon returned with the supplies Adnan requested.

"Everyone back off and give them some room, wouldya?"

Adnan's hands moved with precision. He paused briefly to wipe his hands with the towel and whiskey every few minutes. He grabbed the hands of his patient and pressed them against the ice compress. "Hold this against your neck," he said, standing up. The bar cheered as he straightened his back.

Tim slapped him on his back. "I had no idea you spoke any English, and I really didn't know you were a doctor!"

Adnan smiled. "English not so good. Better doctor."

"Where did you learn to work on a man like that?"

"In combat. In medical school. In practice."

Tim shook his head. "Jaysis, Mary, and Joseph, why didn't you say something?"

"Allah does not like proud and boastful people," Adnan replied, his eyes averted. He felt a tap on his back.

"Thanks for saving my friend," an embarrassed Kilkenny soccer fan said, looking down as his vocal chords lumped up. "I would have let the fecker die after the way we treated you a few minutes ago. Sorry for the trouble."

Adnan smiled.

Grace looked up from her sorry attempts at texting when she heard a loud thump on the hood of the car.

Adnan had crashed into the bumper, aided by Tim O'Malley.

"Turns out yer man is fond of the Guinness after all."

Grace bolted out of the car, wagging her finger.

"Jaysis! The state of yeh! Are you trying to get yourself fired from the only job you were able to get?"

"Ah, yeh may wanna lay off the auld fella," Tim said, tussling Adnan's curly hair as he vomited on the wheel. "He's a hero now!"

Adnan raised his fist in the air as his head rocked back and forth.

"OLE! OLE! OLE! OLE!" he sang into the night air, giggling furtively.

"What in the name of hell is going on?"

"This one saved some Kilkenny eejit from bleeding to death on the floor of my bar," he said with pride. "Mind yeh, the fecker deserved more than that for the shite he was spewing. So, Adnan stopped the bleeding and stitched him up good as new with nothing more than a piece of thread and a whiskey. 'Twas like MacGyver, like. The lads in the pub wanted to thank him in the only way they knew how."

Grace swayed on her feet, taking it all in.

"He's a doctor?"

The wind licked the black and yellow flags of Kilkenny that sat atop of the cloud-like tents hanging over the spectators as the local councilman spoke.

"Nowadays, we seem to be living in a world that is more inclined to build walls between us rather than appreciate our differences."

"Adnan Misri is a man who demonstrated not only true heroics but leadership as well. Leadership is defined as creating opportunities for others to act, and Adnan did that by example, acting selflessly to save another man's life even when that meant swimming in a tide of racism and bigotry. He may not have walked into O'Malley's Bar as an Irishman that day, but by God, he walked out of there an Irishman and an honorary Kilkennyman to boot!"

The crowd rose to its feet and cheered.

Adnan bowed his head as the politician proudly looked on, clapping for a brief moment before continuing with his speech.

"His quick thinking and excellent stitching not only saved the life of our star player, it also sewed him into the faculty at University Hospital Galway, where he will care for the unique needs of our Muslim brethren living among us. Now, it is with deep appreciation, on behalf of the Irish people, that I present you with *An Bonn Míleata Calmachta le hOnóir*, Ireland's Medal for Gallantry with Honour."

The church ladies of Brooklodge Church, all decked out in their Sunday best, fanned out like a brigade toward the gaggle of press tents and satellite dishes.

Fiona and John were waiting in the idling BMW convertible as Adnan and the family drove past their car. Catching Fiona's eye, Adnan asked the driver to stop before rolling down the window.

"Thank you both again for everything you've done for us," Adnan said. Maya circled around the car, and the kids jumped out to hug them around the waist.

Johnny waved dismissively. "Sure, all we did was put a roof over your head. You did the rest on your own," he replied, averting his eyes.

Adnan shook his head. "You can be humble all you want. But we'll never forget you."

The families finished hugging one another before Adnan shepherded his brood back into the car. Johnny unlocked the car and started to walk around the driver's side when Fiona grabbed him by the arm. She was slumped against the car, a twisted expression plastered across her face.

"Are you okay?" Johnny asked as he grabbed her arm.

"I just lost my footing in this wet grass, I suppose. Maybe it was just all the excitement of the day."

"Well, which one is it?"

"It's nothing," Fiona said closing her eyes. "Nothing a strong cup of tea wouldn't fix. Let's go.

CHAPTER 4

CARRIAGE HOUSE 3: THE REPORTER

"This looks like the place," Peter Schatz said to the pleasant female voice on the GPS app of his phone that he had named Blanche as it announced that he had arrived at his destination. He navigated the small Audi A4 hatchback through the tight portal that led into the carriage house square. A blanket of predawn fog licked the tires as he made his way up the winding driveway toward the guest houses. He parked in front of Carriage House 3 and got out.

"Jesus, you half expect the Headless Horseman to come out of that grove of trees to slice your head," he muttered to himself. The column of his 56-year-old spine creaked as he bent down, removed the key from underneath the mat as per Fiona's emailed instructions, and let himself in.

To his right was a small table with a plate of soda bread and butter covered in clear plastic. It had a rustic crust that reminded him of the breads his grandmother made, though these seemed to have raisins dotted across the coarse landscape. A tea and coffee service was next to an electric kettle. There was a card propped against the plate that simply said "welcome" in handwritten block letters.

The air carried a faint smell of lemon cleaner. He looked around at the knotty, lacquered wood floors, which looked newly renovated and matched the stairwell and the legs of the sparse dormitory furniture meticulously. Jet lag hung on his shoulders like a lead bib. All he wanted to do was sleep, yet the smell of bacon that wafted from the window of the main house made his stomach rumble with anticipation.

He dropped his bags in the room and climbed up the stairs into the bathroom to wash away the film of dirt he imagined on his face after being on a plane for nine hours. The cold water on his face jolted him momentarily from the molten exhaustion that seeped into his bones. He tucked the stray shirt collar back into his black V-neck sweater, flicked the lint from his broad chest as he looked in the mirror, and tucked the runaway strands of thick gray hair behind his ear before making his way back down the stairs and over toward the main house.

Fiona watched him walking over. He was a broad and handsome cut of a man, she thought. Though his face was heavily creased with acne scars, he had a long square jaw that jutted out from beneath a generous mane of tousled hair. He revealed intense green eyes when he removed his dark Ray-Ban sunglasses and knocked on the door.

"You're very welcome," Fiona said as she opened the door. They shook hands.

"Thank you. I'm Peter, and I must say, this place is even more beautiful than the pictures online."

"Ah, thanks," Fiona said proudly. "We try our best. Did you find everything okay?"

Peter nodded. His investigative reporter mind began scanning the details of the main house and the woman standing before him. The lush décor blended slim antique tables with plush modern leather couches. She was up this early looking this good, which pointed to a woman driven; she had probably been a high-powered executive once. *There's no way she could have made all this cash by peddling rooms online,* he thought.

"It was great," he replied. "Thanks. I can't wait to dig into the soda bread!"

"Would you have a little tea? The breakfast is almost ready," she replied.

"Every molecule in my being wants to just collapse right now, but I couldn't resist the aroma."

"That trip over is terrible, isn't it? I tell ya, you're not right for the first few days with the jet lag. What airport did you fly out of?"

"JFK," he replied. "Getting there from the city is an adventure in and of itself."

Fiona nodded. "Didn't I make that trip a million times myself over the years before I got married? That Belt Parkway is murder at any hour. Do you live in the city?"

"I do," Dan replied. "I work for *The New York Daily Times.*"

Fiona's brows peaked. "Really? That's grand. Sure, I always wanted to write. What brings you out here?"

Peter looked at her in disbelief. "I see the newspaper near the mug of tea there on the table. I think the answer to the question is there on the front page."

Fiona offered a polite smile. "Well, there goes my hopes of a feature in *The New York Daily Times* travel section I suppose."

Peter laughed. "You always wanted to write. Well, I always wanted to be a travel writer. Those guys seem like they have so much more fun than hardened news guys like me.

I always regretted not writing in a more descriptive, artistic style that the travel pieces seem to need."

"I must admit to reading your work, and I am a huge fan," she replied calmly. "Nothing wrong with your writing; I'd say you'd be a marvelous travel writer."

"That's nice of you to say, and thanks for reading my work. Who knows? Maybe your fine establishment could change my ways. I'm happy to pass along the great experiences I've had so far to the editor and see where it goes. I am definitely impressed with what I've seen."

"Thanks. I'd imagine it would be a cheerier read than these headlines," Fiona said with a tiny sigh. "They're hard to look at, and each day's paper brings with it another atrocity."

"I would imagine they are," Peter replied. "One thing I am glad I am not? A political reporter. I don't know how those guys do it with this current Oval Office."

"I'd say there's no shortage of things to write about, and you don't have to go far for a story since he is so blatant about twisting the truth."

"Have you lived in this area all your life?"

"I'm from Sligo, which is north a bit. This is my husband's farm. He was born and raised here. This farm provided eggs and milk to businesses around here back in the day."

Peter raised his eyebrow. "Is that so? Did his family see anything strange when they made their deliveries at the convent in Tuam where they buried those babies' bodies in the backyard?"

Fiona pouted. "I have no comment either way and don't bother asking the man of the house. You'll get even less from him."

"People have a way of opening up around me. Might be my sparkling personality, or maybe it's the dimples."

Fiona smirked. "Good luck peddling that around Tuam," she replied. "You'll find they're the type of people who shun the spotlight and keep to themselves. Of course, the Sligo crowd, on the other hand."

Peter's eyes narrowed. "Okay, so I get that, and I get that you don't have any working knowledge of what went on in that orphanage in Tuam. But just, you know, Catholic to Catholic, what are your feelings about it? Off the record of course."

"Of course," Fiona nodded warily. "Well, it's a complicated situation. On the surface, obviously, it's a scourge against humanity that they disposed of human remains on the property in such a way. That may boggle the mind to a Yank like yourself, and I'm not defending it, of course. Then again, you have to put the activity in its proper time and place."

"Ms. Burke, how do you put the Bon Secours nuns disposing of the bodies of babies in their care into a drainage ditch in its proper place?"

Fiona straightened her chair. "From the sound of it, it would seem you already wrote your article on the plane ride over here," she replied icily. "Call me naïve, but I expect a little more from *The New York Daily Times* in times like these."

"Well, it looks like I lost a fan." He leveled a gaze at her, ready for anything.

She tapped on her iPad. "I'm sorry. We have Wifi here in the bog, believe it or not. I never miss your column. I'm a huge fan, and I was so excited to see your reservation come through, though my stomach has been flipping with nerves at the thought of what you'd do to this story."

Peter leaned in and fumbled for his pocket tape recorder. "How so?"

Fiona looked down disapprovingly. "You said this was off the record. It's probably not a bad idea to warn you at this point that I'm a solicitor with an active license who's not afraid to use it."

"Solicitor?"

Fiona chuckled. "Sorry. In Ireland, we call lawyers solicitors."

"Whoa, whoa, calm down," Peter said reassuringly. "I wasn't going to put you on the record. I was just going to make some mental notes for myself."

Her cell phone chirped, announcing a text. Fiona excused herself, stood up from the kitchen table, and went to her phone.

Guest arrive OK? Johnny texted.

Yes. He's already starting with the questions. Mind what you say around him, she replied and hit send.

"Mr. Schatz, if you don't mind, let me finish serving up your breakfast, and then I do need to help my husband on the farm. I assume it will be a bed you want straight away after a long journey, but if you want a shower first, the towels are in the shelves above the toilet." Fiona stopped on the stairs. "If you want to get a unique perspective on the Tuam convent story, you might want to try my friend Mattie Fahey. His family runs the butcher shop in town; they've had that business for 100 years. They're connected to that place in some unique ways."

Peter's eyes brightened. "Thank you."

With a nod, she was gone. He thought she knew so much more, and there was so much she could have said and didn't. She was clearly guarded and trained as a lawyer to just answer the question, so there would be no slip of the tongue from that one. Peter quickly finished his breakfast, moved the dishes to the sink, and walked across the square. He collapsed onto the bed with his clothes still on and proceeded to sleep for the next five hours.

He snaked the car through the fields and followed the GPS navigation prompts into Tuam. He circled for parking for a few minutes and was soon advised by a pedestrian to go to the back lot of the Corey Court Hotel in the center of town because the main street would be clogged with shoppers at the noon hour. It was a clean, whitewashed four-story building in the center of town, a stone arch between its buildings guarding a small parking lot. He parked the car and went inside. The lacquered floor of the dining area reflected the brilliant autumn sunlight that perforated the delicate and worn lace curtains on the window. There was a bar to the left, and it was sparsely populated with the occasional bar patron hunched over both his pint and cell phone at the bar. His eyes locked with those of the nervous-looking older man in the corner. He was dressed in a simple V-neck navy sweater with a powder-blue shirt collar and a navy necktie peering through.

Peter's tough exterior melted at the sight of him. Not many people in his line of work dressed up in their Sunday best to be interviewed. He liked the man immediately.

Mattie's knotty hands were those of a butcher, and they fumbled with the end of the napkin. Peter nodded his head, and the man nodded back. He stood up as Peter approached the table, introduced himself as Mattie Fahey, and gingerly offered a hand in greeting just as a pimply teenaged girl scurried to the table and took their coffee orders. Peter took his phone out of the side pocket in his tweed jacket, activated the recorder app, and placed the phone between them. Mattie's fatigued blue eyes followed his every move.

"You're okay if I record this?" Peter asked.

"I am," he said. "Though I think I might talk a little better if this wasn't staring me in the face, like. Mind if we put it to the side a bit or throw a napkin over it?"

Peter nodded with a smile. There was a sadness that saturated this man. He knew this look; this man came to unburden his soul. Peter made a mental note to downshift his blunt approach into a more compassionate tone. "Of course. Whatever makes you feel comfortable. So, what's your connection to the Bon Secours Home for Women and Babies?"

"Not so much me but 'twas my family," he replied. "I'm 75 years of age, so a lot of what went on happened when I was small. My sister Margaret had more to do with that place."

"Where is your sister now?"

"She's gone, Lord have mercy on her soul."

Peter nodded briefly. "Sorry for your loss."

"It's okay. 'Twas a while ago now that she's gone. She lived in America just across the river from New York in a place called Jersey City."

Peter cut her off. "Get out! I live there now! Grew up there. What was her married name?"

"Schatz. Her Irish name is Mairead Fahey. You Yanks would have called her Margaret. Anyways, she married a German fella with a name much like yours."

The blood ran from Peter's face. "That's because Margaret Schatz is my aunt by marriage. Bob Schatz is my cousin. "

Mattie sat up. "I thought your name was just a coincidence; there are a million people with that name in

Germany and the States. What a small world!" Mattie brought a mug of tea to his lips. "He's got kids in college now, and the fares over are very dear, so I don't see much of him. You'll probably see him before I do, so give him our best from Polsellagh."

"Why do I get the feeling you raising your hand to Fiona that you'd be willing to talk to me is not a coincidence?" Peter replied.

"I suppose it wasn't. I was a bit curious."

"How was your sister connected to the Bon Secours nuns?"

Mattie frowned. He smoothed the widow's peak of thin dyed black hair. "Margaret found herself with child and unmarried. My father sent her to the home, but she was one of the lucky ones. My father, Darby, wanted her there just long enough to have the baby and when that was done, he came to collect her."

Peter paused for a second. His head was shaking slightly. This woman having a child out of wedlock in the conservative Ireland of the 1950s was completely at odds with the woman he was picturing in his mind: the square-looking mom with the green shamrock apron always around her neck and no awareness of how it clashed with what she was wearing at the time. He remembered staying at their house and kneeling on the hard floor at night for a forced family prayer around the parents' bed before the lights were turned off for the evening, something his slacker Catholic parents never bothered to do.

"What happened to the baby?"

Mattie shrugged his shoulders. "We don't really know. There were loads of Yanks coming over from America, and they were all mad for Irish babies. They cleaned many of the orphanages out of the little ones, so if the little fella survived that place, he's probably a few years older than you living his life in America."

"You never saw the boy after he was born?"

"Well, I didn't," Mattie replied, his voice quivering. "But Margaret, Lord have mercy on her, would sneak into town every chance she got to see if she could catch a glimpse of the child."

"I can tell by the emotion of your voice that this is still raw for you."

"Why wouldn't it be? I'm a father myself. A grandfather, in fact. That would just rip me apart. I can't imagine dropping my daughter into a place like that and never seeing my grandchild again, but I suppose that's the way it was in that place and time."

Peter looked up. "You're the second one who has said that to me today: 'It was in that place and time.' Like it justifies it."

"It does," Mattie said flatly.

"Elaborate."

"You have to understand that this was in the Fifties. In those days, the Catholic Church was more powerful than it is today. The priests would be up there on a Sunday talking about the sins of the flesh, and everyone in the pew, your neighbors, would be sitting up and taking notice. They'd notice, for instance, if your daughter was getting a bit thick in the middle. People would start to talk. Maybe people would stop buying your eggs and your cattle because you ran a loose house. Now, I'm not saying that was right, but that's the way it was, right or wrong."

Peter sat back. "So, your father caved under the pressure of what the neighbors would think?"

"That was part of it but the other part was about losing his business if people stopped supporting his business," Mattie replied. "Again, it was the way it was and still is, I suppose. Margaret didn't see it that way. She would get to the Bon Secours Home for Women and Babies every chance she got. One time, my mother caught her hanging on the steel gate, wailing and crying. She dragged her into the car and beat the living hell out of her when she got home. Within two weeks, she was shipped off to America to live with my mother's sister."

Peter winced. His mind went back to a time when he was five; he was caught in a torrential rain on the way to her house from school because both parents worked. She went out to find him and, instead of belittling him as his father would, his aunt gave him a reassuring hug right in the middle of the rain storm. "Jesus. That's harsh. Poor Aunt Margaret."

"Harsh like your judgment," Mattie replied, circling the rim of the tea mug with his index finger. "Again, you have to remember the time. I'm not angry at my mother and father for what they did. At least, not anymore."

"Did she ever see the boy?"

Mattie reached under his sweater and pulled out a small black and white photo. He slid it across the table. Peter looked at the grainy picture of a child sitting up in a pram looking at the camera; it looked as though the picture was taken through the bars of a gate.

"Is this the boy? Who took the photo?"

Mattie nodded. "We think it is. Well, Margaret insisted it was anyway. We were too poor to afford a camera back in those days, but one of her fancy girlfriends in town had one. She paid the girl to take it. She had two copies of that picture. One was under her pillow, and, when my parents sent her away, she left this one behind with my other sister. She told us to keep looking for him in Ireland, and she would do the same in America. I could hear enough of the yelling that came through the door when she was with my mother and father to know what was going on."

"Unbelievable."

"It was."

"Then why come forward? Why now?"

"For Margaret. She went off to America, got a job in a supermarket, met the German fella..."

"My dad's brother, Otto," Peter interrupted.

"She did, and she started a new life for herself like the brave girl she was," he said with a nod. "She had two fine kids, Bobby being one of them, and when she'd bring the lot of them over after my parents died, she was all smiles. But I know my sister. There was a piece of her missing."

"You're hoping to find this piece?"

"I am. My heart is in bits when I think of all the babies buried on that property. Not sure if we'll ever know if our little fella is buried there, but I'd like to think he isn't and that I'll live to see the day when he comes back to his family."

Peter sat silent for a moment. He thought of his stoic cousin Bob; how would he react to this kind of news? If it were him, he'd be overjoyed to find out about a sibling he didn't know he'd had; he was sure he'd get a good book out of it. With Bob, it was hard to tell. "Does my cousin know?"

"I don't think so," Mattie said sheepishly. "It was something I thought wasn't my news to tell for the longest time. Margaret swore me to secrecy, and I honored that for years, even when Bob would come back for an occasional visit over the years without his mother. But now these news reports are starting to come out, and they're bringing up all kinds of memories for me. I feel a bit guilty for keeping the secret all the same."

“I can imagine,” Peter said, his mind churning out the next question. He looked at the heartbroken old man in front of him, and he began to regret all the judgment he had packed in this trip. “I’d like to contact Bob to see if there is anything from his mother that I can pick up to help piece some of this together.”

Mattie winced. “It’d be kinda awkward if we just spring this on him. Maybe I should make contact with him first? I think it’s best he hear it from me.”

Peter nodded. “I know that won’t be an easy call to make, but it will be the right thing to do.”

With that, the focus on his story shifted. Fiona Burke was right: he had begun writing the narrative on the plane ride over from New York. He was convinced a new take on the story would be in some alley under some rock not turned over by a local country bumpkin newshound here. Hadn’t he learned anything from the great Jimmy Breslin’s classic interview with James Winners, the gravedigger who buried JFK? Breslin always makes a story where no one else was looking. The story was right in front of him now—he would use his investigative skills to find out what happened to Aunt Margaret’s baby. But first, his editor back home was expecting his first serving of raw red meat, so he went back to Crumlin Manor, fished the soda bread from its plastic wrap confines on the kitchen table, and began writing his first in a series of columns.

"House of Horrors:" Shining a Light on a Catholic Home for Women and Babies
By Peter Schatz, *The New York Daily Times*, March 15, 2017

Darby Fahey started out as a farmer but ended up a butcher and a salesman.

He would carefully arrange the colorful assortment of meats, fruits, and vegetables in boxes at either side of the display that resembled the pitch of a house on the back of his pickup truck, being careful to put the candies at the bottom to attract the impulsive children as their parents fretted over the ingredients for this week's dinner.

It was the postwar Fifties, and this man's business was built on relationships with every family on the narrow roads in and around the very Catholic enclave of Corrofin in County Galway, Ireland. The news of an unmarried teenage daughter at home would have clouded those relationships and shriveled his business like a sundried tomato. Like hundreds of men in his position, Fahey took his daughter to the nuns at the Bon Secours Home for Women and Babies in nearby Tuam. This town on the other side of the county would be just far enough away from the prying eyes of his customers.

"He didn't feel like he had a choice, and indeed, he didn't," his son, Mattie, now 75, recalls as we chat in a Tuam pub 64 years later. "His customers would have shunned our family, and my father couldn't risk that."

The Home operated a laundry on the premises; it was where these pregnant, unmarried teen mothers would scrub the impossibly stubborn stains of imaginary sins from their souls.

Margaret Fahey was one of those girls, but she was one of the lucky ones. Many families left their daughters to rot inside the gates of the Home, but Darby collected Margaret as soon as the baby was born, after she had lost most of the post-delivery weight. The baby wouldn't leave the Home until two years later, when an American family came and adopted Margaret's son.

"This was big business back then," recalls John McDonald, 80, a former priest who now lives with his partner in Tuam. "Infertile families looking for 'the Gerber babies,' as the Yanks called them; you know, the wee one whose picture was on the cereal box. They fetched a nice price for the nuns, who used the money to fund an endless river of baby formula and clothes. The locals thought they were doing the Lord's work and paid no mind to what was going on inside the walls."

Behind those black wrought iron gates was a horror show; babies, ravaged by malnutrition and felled by incurable diseases such as measles and mumps, were unceremoniously dumped in drainage ditches and buried ten feet deep. Only the prettiest were quarantined from the rest of the population because they would be the ones to generate the most income when the Americans came calling. The children were taken from the arms of mothers, often children themselves, with a cold-bloodedness that contradicts the namesake of the nuns (the literal French translation of Bon Secours is "good help," and their motto is "good help to those in need").

Mattie recalls the day his sister came home after witnessing her baby being taken out of the Home. "She had this faraway look in her eyes, like the light of her life was extinguished from them. Every corner held a memory that haunted her, and I think she was being driven mad. Of course, no one knew or talked about post-partum depression in those days, and I'm sure she was dealing with that on top of anything else. It was too painful for her to stay here, so she left for America and rarely came home after that."

Though the actions of the nuns seem barbaric to most, Sr. Philomena Donahue, a spokeswoman for Stand Up For Catholics, a watchdog group defending their church from naysayers, has a different perspective. "You have to put what happened in their proper context," she asserts. "Burying stillborn babies on the farm was not uncommon in that area during that time. In fact, there is a plaque in the local cemetery erected recently to honor those souls known as 'lisheen babies' in and around the Tuam area. Yes, I know the idea of burying 796 babies in the drainage ditch sounds horrific, and, in this day and age, it is. But we're not talking about this day and age, and liberal, sensational rags like The New York Daily Times *never bother to point that out."*

Mattie Fahey doesn't disagree with those facts, but he still holds the nuns accountable for behavior he deems at odds with the Catholic values his own father held so dear. "Those babies were never baptized," he says, his voice cracking under the weight of hurt and anger. "These so-called charitable nuns didn't deem these children worthy of love, so they were segregated in their own classes in school. I just can't imagine growing up with that kind of rejection all your life."

Mattie considers his family among the lucky ones; he says his father had the good sense to pull Margaret from the Home rather than sentence her to a life of church slavery, and he has reason to believe his nephew escaped the fate of burial in a septic tank. Eyewitnesses claimed the boy was adopted by an American family at the age of 2.

"I hope that family gave the little fella a good life," he says wistfully. "He may have been taken from our family, but we never forgot about him. If he ever makes it back to Ireland, he's welcome in my house at any time."

Fiona smiled and blinked back a tear as she finished the article on her iPad, just as Peter came into the main house. "I just read your piece in the paper."

"What did you think of it?"

"I think it's amazing how you can file a story from across the courtyard, email it into your editor in Manhattan, and I can be reading it from across the courtyard in *The New York Daily Times* an hour later. The immediacy of journalism nowadays..."

"Okay then," he said with a laugh. "There's my answer."

Fiona smiled. "I told you, I am a huge fan of your work. This is an excellent piece as usual, and it's right on target. It's just, you know, a little hard to read about my town in general and my church in particular under these circumstances."

Peter nodded as he poured his coffee. "Being a reporter means getting stricken off of more Christmas card lists and gala invites than you can shake a stick at. How well do you know Mattie Fahey?"

"I know his wife from church," she answered. "Mattie's a wonderful and gentle man who has been a friend of mine for years. Mattie was a great footballer in the upper classes when Johnny was younger and they went to school together. Johnny even dated one of Mattie's sisters at one point."

Peter perked up. "Was it Margaret?"

"Good Lord, no!" Fiona exclaimed. "It was Anne Marie. Margaret was about 20 years older than the pair of them. No, she was out of here at 16, so I'm told."

"Does anybody remember what reasons she gave for leaving so young?"

Fiona shrugged. "It was nothing unusual. You have to understand that there was absolutely nothing here for young people in the Fifties; the war had decimated much of Europe, which was one of Ireland's biggest trade partners. Just desperate times. Many girls her age left the first chance they got."

"There seemed to be more to the story than that, according to Mattie."

"Why the interest in Margaret all of a sudden?"

"Well, this story; it's a bit personal now. Margaret was my aunt by marriage. I never knew her maiden name; she was just the Irish Auntie Margaret from my childhood. I really loved that woman. According to Mattie, his sister was forced to give a baby out of wedlock into the Bon Secours Home for Women and Babies, and no one knew what happened to him. She was apparently heartbroken and left for America to start a new life for herself."

Fiona shook her head. "You knew Margaret? Imagine that. I hadn't realized."

"I hadn't either," Peter said. Freaky coincidence."

"The poor thing. Is there anyone else in town that could help me find out more about the son?"

"As a matter of fact, my law firm worked with *The Irish Daily Times*, your partner paper, to draw up the first subpoenas to the Archdiocese of Tuam to release those records. The church fought it tooth and nail, but after a few leaks to the press, the court of public opinion was on our side. Of course, the fact that people started to reduce the money into the church basket on Sunday as a result of the articles we planted didn't hurt the cause as well."

"That's a clever use of the press."

"When you're on the right side of them, reporters can be a useful tool," she replied. "I've been on the wrong side of them in cases I've carried over the years, so I know the downside of the buggers as well, no offense." She curtsied before heading to the table and scribbling a name and number on a sheet of paper. "We copied all of the birth and death records and kept PDFs for an old case against the church in general, and that place in particular, for something along the lines of what you're pursuing. Our clerk Dara will be able to give you access to them. I'll text her to let her know you'll be in to the office later today so that she'll have everything ready for you."

There was a knock on the door. Fiona looked up and smiled at the old man at the window. He was gaunt in his crisp white uniform and matching cap. Tufts of white hair that curled upward seemed indistinguishable from the hat itself. She threw open the door. "Howaya, Jimmy! Come in for a cuppa tea."

He shuffled a few steps into the kitchen. "I will, so, Missus. This is my last stop of the day." Behind him was a handcart stacked with cartons of eggs, cases of milk, and boxes of cheese.

"I haven't seen a milkman in years," Peter exclaimed, offering his hand. "What a treat! Pleased to meet you. My name is Peter."

"Jimmy Rooney—you must be the reporter fella," Jimmy said, shaking Peter's hand. "I heard you were asking some questions about the Bon Secours Home in town earlier today."

"How did you hear?"

"The man hears and sees all," she snickered. "He can't drive 30 feet without someone offering him tea and a secret along the route."

"Been doing it for almost sixty years," Jimmy said with pride.

Peter looked at him intently. "Tell me, Jimmy: was the Bon Secours Home part of your milk run."

"'Twas," he replied. "At one point, they were the biggest customer. We'd all line up at the crack of dawn when the Reverend Mother would come into the back kitchen to make the day's orders. There'd be no less than six of us in line, and if you were late for the appointment, by Jesus, she'd give you nothing."

"How well did you know her?"

"Well enough, I suppose. You kept your head down and asked no questions to a woman like that, just talked when you were spoken to. Maybe it was the fear that they beat into you when you were in school yourself. Who knows?"

"Did you see anything during your time there?"

Jimmy hesitated, looking in Fiona's direction for approval. She nodded. "Bits and pieces," he continued cautiously. "You'd see a child shuffling around, his eyes glassy, like he was battling something. Young girls would be sent over to the laundries to do work, and the kids would sorta be walking around."

"Why didn't you say anything if you were suspicious of something?"

"You have to understand the time," the old man replied, thumping the table with his hand. "The media is sensationalizing this, like we were all protecting the church or turning a blind eye. We considered the priests and sons to be doing Christ's work. They were special. Call it naïve if you want, but to be suspicious of them was like being suspicious of Christ himself. That's the part you lot don't seem to get."

"I see," Peter replied. "I was talking to Mattie Fahey this morning, and he had mentioned that one of his sisters had a son in that home."

"I remember the day that nice family took the child away from that God forsaken place," Jimmy replied, closing his eyes. "They came in one of those fancy black rental cars that we didn't see very often in these parts. Mother Superior was all smiles when the envelope of cash was placed in her hand for 'the continuing work of the church' as she'd call it. Anyway, I can still hear poor Margaret screaming and running after the car when someone at the gate told her that the baby was gone. A man can't ever forget a thing like that."

"I suppose you wouldn't," Fiona replied, wiping the inside of a washed tea mug with a towel as she spoke. "Isn't that terrible?"

Peter turned to Jimmy. "So, Jimmy, you can verify that you saw the baby leave the premises safely?"

"I did," he replied. "That was 64 years ago, fourteenth of May, 1953 because it was my mammy's last birthday with us. I remember like it was yesterday."

"This has been a huge help," Peter said before standing up and shaking Jimmy's hand again. "I'm going to go back into town and interview a few more people."

Peter drummed his fingers on the steering wheel as he navigated his car through the narrow roads leading to Tuam. The pride each of the owners took on their storefronts was evident; the stucco faces painted in a myriad of muted pastel colors created a vibrant rainbow that lined the thin and clogged streets in the center of town.

Dara was at the front door of the law office. They shook hands, exchanged pleasantries centered around how awesome Fiona was, and walked into a conference room where a laptop and a coffee service awaited Peter.

"All of the records are on the thumb drive in the laptop," Dara said. "You're free to use the office for as long as you want."

Peter pored through the files and was sickened by what he saw. Hundreds of babies were logged into the records of the church, and at least one in three passed away from preventable diseases likes measles and mumps. True, many of the medicines taken for granted today weren't available back then, but it was hard to imagine quarantine measures were taken to save the babies in the nuns' care.

After two hours of bleary-eyed review of the files, he found two names of babies, both boys, birthed by women named Margaret Fahey. They were two months apart, ruling out the possibility that the same woman would have given birth to both children. One of the babies was given to a couple, Blake and Michelle Lambert. The registry called the boy "Caoimhín," meaning kind, honest, and handsome in the Gaelic tongue. "Kevin" is the English translation of the name.

The first letter of the state abbreviation was smudged beyond recognition but the last letter was an "A." California, Massachusetts, Virginia, Washington, possibly Pennsylvania?

He sent emails to the newsrooms of *The Boston Globe* and *The Washington Post* and asked these affiliates for support in researching any Lambert families who had adopted babies from Ireland. He then leveraged some law enforcement contacts he had from Florida in the past year when he followed the President down to Mar-a-Lago in West Palm Beach during the campaign. He was about to close down his laptop when his mobile phone buzzed. He had it on silent and missed a call from someone local. He activated his voicemail messages.

"Mr. Schatz, it's Mattie Fahey. I just got off the phone with Bob from America, and I told him the news. I pointed him to the article you wrote as well. I'd say he was in a bit of shock, but as I said, better to hear it from me I suppose. Anyway, you're free to call him whenever you'd like."

Peter changed his flight online, drove back to Crumlin Manor, and packed his belongings because the story now resided in America. At the airport, he uploaded another column to the newsroom.

The Bon Secours Home for Women and Babies: The Gateway to Hell
Opinion By Peter Schatz, *The New York Daily Times*, March 17, 2017

Margaret Fahey was a fine woman married to my father's brother. She immigrated to Ireland in the 1950s, and, despite being heavily outnumbered by the Germans all around her, she injected much-appreciated Irish culture into our family. Every St. Patrick's Day, after the remnants of corned beef and cabbage were scrubbed from the plates that soaked in her sink, my cousin Bob and I would sit at her feet and watch The Quiet Man, *starring John Wayne and Maureen O'Hara.*

One of the earliest and fondest memories my Aunt Margaret had centered around catching shillings on the train tracks that John Wayne threw out to her and the other star-struck local kids on the set.

There is a cruel irony that The Quiet Man, *the most beloved movie in Irish culture, would be filmed in and around Tuam, a town that kept quiet about burying babies in the backyard even while the movie was being made.*

The horrific news reports out of the town I've walked around these past few days are so hard to bear that I have no interest in rehashing them here in this space. But there are some key omissions in the narrative that are worth calling out.

In following this story, I haven't seen or heard anyone address the termites in the floorboard of Irish DNA that made the very existence of a home for unwed mothers and babies necessary in the first place.

What no one is saying is that the Irish culture of looking good in front of the neighbors built every brick in that slice of hell on earth within Tuam, and the conditions of overcrowding occurred because the demand to hide the perceived "family embarrassment" overwhelmed the nuns. By dropping their frightened and disowned daughters at the gate, the parents were asking the nuns to bury the problem. Who is to blame if the good Sisters of Bon Secours (that's French for "good health," by the way) carried out their customers' commands in the most literal sense?

No one is talking about how it takes a village to hide something of this magnitude. I'm sure the home reached outside the walls for people to deliver milk, turf and food, making the thousands of people serving homes like this one culpable in these crimes by their silence. Indeed, I heard plenty of stories from people damning those young girls in their judgments and smugly making the sign of the cross at the gate, thanking their Maker that their own daughters would never put their family through any red-faced shame in the village.

Yes, some of the Irish news outlets, reacting to the understandable public outrage, are rightly calling for a church investigation into the deaths that occurred for decades at the home for unwed mothers run by the Bon Secours nuns in Tuam. With their Twitter feeds and Facebook pages, the Irish around the world are now the villagers at the gates of the Catholic Church with their keyboards being the equivalent of pitchforks and torches. It is easier to do that than to look inward and measure our own cultural character flaws that created this scourge on our race.

As a German American, I have some experience of that on my shores. I remember vividly how a family friend of ours sent a daughter to a semester away at college when she found herself "in the family way."

The girl had a son by herself and then worked off the baby weight as part of her brother's landscaping business to ensure she was fit and trim in September like nothing ever happened. We didn't find out about it until decades later, when the son emerged triumphant a few years back with a blue ribbon in a Manhattan one-act play festival for telling his life story in a humorous way.

Minister for Education Ruairi Quinn said he broadly supports calls for a full inquiry into all mother-and-baby homes but then tried to downplay the blight that's making the entire nation look pitiful on the world stage. "These things need to be looked at in the context of their time," he said. I've heard that phrase a lot this week.

Is that so? What happened is that the remains of 800 children were unceremoniously buried in a drainage ditch, no less. How can you mistake that for anything other than an atrocity and a total breakdown in humanity?

It is early goings in the scandal; I get that. I don't have the strength and level of faith to raise my hand and make the sign of the cross at the moment, but when and if I get there, I will pray that Ireland transforms this obsession with looking good into something that resembles authenticity and dignity for the human spirit.

Peter parked the car on the steep side street just off Kennedy Boulevard in Jersey City, making sure to jam the parking brake so the rented Zipcar wouldn't roll away. He eased into Narrowbacks, the small bar at the fork in the road between the pathway into New York City and the immigrant enclave known as the Heights section.

Bob Schatz was seated on a barstool toward the back of the bar, and he nodded when he saw his cousin enter. Bob was all German, his long, pointed nose holding up the thin framed square glasses near his translucent eyebrows.

At 64, there wasn't a wrinkle on his skin, but he looked considerably older than Peter remembered nonetheless.

After a brief hug, the pair sat on adjoining barstools and Peter ordered a scotch and soda. "Well, you were a busy boy in Ireland," Bob snickered. "Way to upend a guy's fucking life."

"Journalism isn't pretty," Peter deadpanned. "You are joking, I assume. I mean, I went over there to do a job on that orphanage from hell over in Tuam. I had no idea I would run into your uncle and certainly never imagined I'd dig something up on Aunt Margaret."

Bob shrugged, puffed up his cheeks, and slowly let the air out.

"Well, now we have it all out in the open for millions of people to know now. Ah, who gives a shit?"

"I can imagine it's weird for you."

Bob turned his body toward Peter, who flinched because he was convinced a punch was about to be thrown. "Can you? Can you imagine? Really? One minute you're just minding your own business and then, bam! You have to read in the paper that your cousin has told your uncle a secret life that your mother led! Now I have a brother. A brother! Jesus!"

Peter lowered his head. "It's a lot to process, I know. I'm here for you. Whatever you need."

"Well, I needed privacy, but I'm sure that's not something I'm gonna fucking get! I can see the story arc now: you'll be following me to meet this guy and then who knows? Why don't we all go over to Ireland and film the reunion?"

Peter fumbled with a business card in his pocket. "Well, now that you mention it..."

Bob looked down.

"This is the phone number of Kevin Lambert of Manassas, Virginia," Peter continued. "I believe he's your brother, Bob. He's agreed to meet us at Union Station in D.C. tomorrow morning."

Bob shook his head. "You are unbelievable! You sure that's going to give you enough time to grab a camera crew, a pen, and a paper? I mean, I don't want to put any pressure on you, bro."

"Come on, man. I'm you're only cousin in the area; you're going to need the support."

"Is that why you're going? Really?" Bob bellowed. "What if I don't want to meet him, huh? Do I have any say in this?"

"Yes, there's a story there, okay? You wake up to put bad guys in jail; it's just what detectives do! "Investigative reporters seek the truth. We're not all that much different."

Bob rolled his eyes. "You're laying it on thick."

"You're not the least bit curious? Your wife left you, and your kids are grown and living far away from here."

"And I need more family. Is that your angle?"

Peter shrugged. "Sure, there's shock here, but let's not lose sight of the fact that you've just gotten the gift of a brother here."

"I'm not sure I want to unwrap it," Bob countered.

Peter reached into his jacket pocket and placed an envelope on the lacquered bar. "It would be a shame to waste these two first-class Amtrak tickets."

"Okay, okay! Jesus!" he retorted.

They said nothing as the Amtrak high-speed Acela rocketed through the New Jersey and Delaware countryside and Bob grazed his big thumbs over the glass of his smart phone. He'd whisper an occasional "Jesus Christ" as he searched through the stories in the Irish press about the Bon Secours Home and the hospital records they attempted to keep from public view. When the conductor announced they were arriving in Baltimore, Bob started to become more agitated and talkative. "So, how did you arrive on the story again?"

"It was the wildest thing. There was a tip into the newsroom about the uncovering of some hospital records in Tuam, and since I had done some work in the church scandals over here, my editor assigned it to me once it was discovered the orphanage was run by the Catholics. It was just a freak coincidence that I would run into your uncle of all people! I mean, I just never made the connection; your mother was always Margaret Schatz, I never knew her maiden name was Fahey."

Bob stroked his chin with one hand. "The detective in me is calling bullshit on the whole thing, just so you know."

Peter leaned in. "How so?"

"The puzzle pieces all came together a little too quickly. The family connection is just a little too close. Out of all the turf cutters in Ireland, the first one you run into is my uncle? That never crossed your mind?"

Before Peter could answer, the conductor came on to announce the train was about to pull into Union Station. Bob exhaled loudly. "Oh, man. What if this guy is a total dick?"

Peter smiled. "Then you will definitely be brothers."

The air brakes hissed below them, and the passengers began to clog the doors. They got up, and it was then that Peter noticed how blotchy the skin around Bob's neck appeared as he wiped his hands on his pants for the tenth time since the train stopped.

"I'm at the Starbucks" was the text Peter received.

They walked gingerly toward the storefront, and what Bob saw made him stop in his tracks. He saw the hands first, the knuckles curled around the paper cup with the middle finger out. He always scolded his mother for holding a cup that way as it appeared she was telling everyone at teatime to screw off. He laughed out loud, a little too hearty for the occasion, as his nerves settled and a boyish enthusiasm took over.

A Sort of Homecoming

By Peter Schatz, *The New York Daily Times*, March 25, 2017

There is a reserved nature of a German, made worse if it is the male species we're dealing with. In fact, the fact that I'm about to write yet another story using a first-person narrative, a no-no for an investigative journalist like myself, makes my flesh crawl.

There were two wary German cousins greeting a very emotional Kevin Lambert, 64, one Saturday morning at a Starbucks in Union Station, in the heart of Washington, D.C. I was one of those Germans, and the other was Lambert's brother, Bob Schatz, who he never knew existed until an article I wrote about a scandal 3,000 miles away in Ireland drew these distant souls together. They had a mother in common; Margaret Fahey had Kevin out of wedlock in rural Catholic Ireland in the 1950s, an imaginary offense punishable by shunning and deep family shame. He spent his first two years in the care of the Bon Secours nuns, proprietors of the Bon Secours Home for Mothers and Babies before the Lamberts rescued him from a life of almost certain premature death due to sickness and malnutrition.

Unbeknownst to the Lamberts, they had also ripped the baby from the arms of his mother, Margaret, who howled in anguish as she clung helplessly to the wrought iron fence as the new family drove away.

"As a parent myself, I cannot imagine the pain this caused her," Kevin Lambert said over coffee, openly weeping. "As an adopted child, there is always a part of you that resents the mother who abandoned you. Knowing this, it gives me great sadness for her but great peace for myself at the same time."

Lambert led an idyllic life in the leafy suburbs of Washington, D.C., with aging parents showering him with affection and a top-notch Jesuit education in an attempt to make up for all those years of childless misery. With a law degree from George Washington University, Lambert chose to work at the National Adoption Center, an advocacy group for adoptive rights.

"It was ironic," he said with a chuckle. "All these years, I wondered what my mother was like, yet what I did for a living was all about guarding the privacy of people like her."

Bob Schatz was raised in a more traditional household, his mother marrying Otto Schatz a year before he was born (full disclosure: Otto is my uncle). He grew up overlooking the Manhattan skyline in Jersey City, with the family subsisting on Otto's meager wages as a bus driver.

"Mom was tough and no-nonsense, but if she loved you, she'd give you the shirt off her back," recalls Schatz. "She kept mostly to herself, but when she was with family, she could be the life of the party. I always felt a sadness in her as I was growing up that I could never put a finger on; now, I know why."

Margaret Schatz died suddenly of an aneurysm two years ago at the age of 79 while walking back from a tai chi class. She opted out of a Christian burial in favor of a simple service on the shoreline along the New Jersey coast, where her ashes were dispersed. "That's one way to get myself back to Ireland," she had joked.

The thirst for any information is clearly insatiable in Lambert, and those details dripped out in a slow trickle from a wary brother trying to make sense of it all. "I still have trouble believing this is my brother, though it's hard to deny my mother's looks and mannerisms that I see in him," said Schatz, 58, a detective set to retire from the Jersey City, New Jersey, police force this June after 30 years of service. "The pointed nose. The hawkish blue eyes. The way he laughs and holds a mug of tea. It's uncanny."

The brothers couldn't be more different in terms of their views of the church institution that tore their family apart. Lambert, a deacon at All Saints Church in Manassas, Virginia, has a deep faith and a reverence to those in religious life. Ironically, Lambert did two tours of duty in a Bon Secours Hospital in Richmond, Virginia, as an intern during his undergraduate studies, when he thought he wanted to be a pediatrician.

Despite their differences, the brothers agreed to a tentative path of getting to know one another. They will bring their children together for their first family gathering in Philadelphia (as a sign of their generation, the cousins have already connected with one another on social media, and their relationship is growing like weeds online) before embarking on a trip to Ireland to visit the Bon Secours Home and Margaret's living brother and sister.

"God has blessed me when I least expected it," a bewildered Kevin Lambert exclaimed as he hugged his "new" 54-year-old brother goodbye. "I know that's a weird thing for a guy like me to say, given how the nuns separated me from my family, but His grace and mercy is undeniable. I could not be happier right now!"

Kevin Lambert was overcome with emotion as he viewed the green patchwork fields of Ireland below him for the first time once the plane breached the cloud line. His daughter Meghan clasped his hand tightly. After collecting their bags and clearing customs, they were shocked to be greeted by a large throng of cheering Irish natives in the waiting area of Shannon Airport.

Both local and national media had latched onto Peter Schatz's stories in *The New York Daily Times* by now, which meant there was a microphone shoved in the direction of the family with every step they took through the terminal. Kevin and Meghan Lambert patiently answered every question before breaking down in a puddle of tears as the Irish Consul General presented them with Irish citizenship. The emotions reached a fever pitch as the crowd parted and allowed Mattie Fahey to embrace his nephew after all these years while cameras whirred around them.

It took them a full hour to wade through the crowd of well-wishers to the car waiting outside. Bob and Peter Schatz were there to greet them at the Crumlin Manor House; they had the good sense to fly in through Heathrow and came into the nearby Knock Airport the night before to avoid the media.

Fiona threw her arms around Kevin and Meghan Lambert as soon as they got out of the car, saving the warmest embrace for her old friend Mattie. They held one another for a long time, the occasional sob escaping from one of them as they swayed.

"I never thought this day would come," Mattie said, wiping his runny nose with a handkerchief. He hobbled over to Bob and gave him a warm handshake followed by a back slap. Mattie looked up at the heavens. "Your mother is up there doing cartwheels, I'm sure!"

Everyone laughed with the exception of Bob, who could only offer a weak smile. He was still suspicious of this, and there was a tinge of jealousy over the fuss his favorite uncle Mattie was making about this new nephew.

"I have a proper Irish breakfast all ready for this gaggle of Yanks. You're very welcome into my home," Fiona exclaimed. She held open the door, and they all filed in one after the other.

They weren't too long after finishing the feast of Irish rashers, eggs, and black pudding when the adrenaline settled and jet lag began to pull on the Lamberts. With a nod of the head, Fiona motioned to Johnny to get up.

"You must be knackered," Johnny said. "I can see it in your faces. Here, let me take you to your cottage. You'll be new people after a few hours of sleep."

Bob got up and pulled his chair back into the table. "I think I'll join you."

They all headed into the courtyard, leaving Peter and Fiona alone in the kitchen. Fiona smiled, collected a pile of plates, and brought them to the sink. As soon as she put them down, Peter began to clap. "Bravo!"

Fiona bowed. "That's nothing. For my next trick, I will mop the floors!"

"That's not what I mean, and you know it," Peter replied, his voice reduced to a growl.

"Excuse me?" Fiona asked, her neck lowering her head into a defensive posture.

"You set this whole thing up. You were the one who contacted *The New York Daily Times* office with an anonymous tip. You were the one who brought Mattie to me. You even brought the old milkman out of the mothballs to add a dash more to this stew you've been stirring on the stovetop this entire time."

"I suppose an overactive imagination comes in handy in your line of work as a journalist, Mr. Schatz?"

"Like the words 'denial' and 'no comment' come in handy in your line of work as a solicitor, Ms. Burke."

"Touché," she countered. "As I've said before, when you're on the right side of them, reporters can be a useful tool."

"Well, congratulations. You pulled the wool over the eyes of *The New York Daily Times.*"

"You sound wounded. Why? My friend got answers to questions that have been haunting him, and that has brought on hard-fought peace in his soul. You got a series of articles that, in my humble opinion as a longtime reader of yours, ranks up there with your finest work. Everyone wins!"

"Just like that in a nice, tiny bow," Peter retorted. "I still have this feeling like I was played all the same. Why me?"

"There was no one but you in my mind the entire time," she replied. "Honest. You are relentless in your pursuit of the story. You are always fair, and you present both sides. Plus, I always get my man. Ask my husband!"

Peter couldn't help but laugh. "I guess I should be flattered."

Fiona winked. "You should be. And proud. Your stories were brilliant, and it completely changed the lives of the people in your family. I'm sure it will inspire other people in a similar situation to step forth and seek the truth. If you're not proud of yourself, well, I am."

Peter started walking toward the door. "Must be the jet lag coming back for round two. I'm too tired to argue with you."

As Fiona watched him walk out, she spotted the priest's car pulling up to the carriage houses. She was whistling the melody of a Clancy Brothers tune as she gathered the dirty dishes and loaded them into the sink. She cupped one hand at the end of the table and swept the bread crumbs into the curled palm with the other. When everything looked to her exacting standards, she reached for the warm mug of tea next to the sink. She was halfway through the first sip when the liquid went down the wrong pipe, setting off a chain reaction of steady coughing. Fiona reached for a paper towel and continued to cough fitfully. When it subsided, she looked down into the towel and gasped when she saw the fresh crimson blood that liberally streaked the mucous. Her hand trembled as she unpacked worst-case scenarios from her mind.

Her father always said that no matter how things ever got, prayer would make you feel better. She normally went through the motions of her faith, but in the last few months, she found herself relying on it more. She closed her eyes, blessed herself, wrapped the paper towel into another towel, and threw it in the garbage.

Fiona's worn knees creaked more than usual as she got out of her car. She moved quickly toward the front door of O'Malley's Funeral Parlor. There was a long line extending across the parking lot, which connected the parlor with the pub next door. She could hear the unmistakable laughter of men inside the pub. It was a throaty laugh that bubbled up slowly from the rib cage of the structure before exploding out of the doorway, filling even the room she was walking into. She rolled her eyes at so much merriment this close to a corpse.

The two women in front of her in the line stopped chatting, looked behind them, and smiled in Fiona's direction in unison. Fiona nodded.

They turned their backs on her and soon resumed their conversation. "She was so young, the creature, it's unsettling," said the tall one.

"Cut down in the prime of her life," replied the short one.

"Funny how we think of being in our sixties as the prime of our life, but here we are."

The short one laughed. The pair of them took five steps toward the door, and Fiona followed. They were almost inside, and Fiona decided to check her text messages one more time, out of boredom.

The tall one leaned into the short one and whispered. "'Twas a bit cruel, don't you think, keeping the fact that she was sick from everyone she knew, even her husband?"

"It was of course," hissed the short one. "Giving everyone the shock of their lives when she finally up and dies. Leaving them all wondering why she never said anything to them. The people left behind have more questions than answers. Cruel indeed."

Fiona looked up from her phone, clearly annoyed by the pair of them.

The short one continued. "On the other hand, maybe she just wanted to spare her family the long agony of going down the road with her."

"Och, sure, that's a complete load of shite," scoffed the tall one. "I mean, really, you know that you're at the end of the road, and after years of loving your family, you shut them out like that? I can't imagine the burden on herself. She probably made herself sicker toward the end holding all of that in."

Fiona couldn't take it anymore, clearing her throat before tapping the short one on the shoulder. "So, are you a doctor? A psychologist, maybe? I'm trying to figure out what makes you so qualified to weigh in on matters like this?"

The short one looked over her shoulder.

"I knew her better than anyone, sure," Fiona continued, "That woman always had her family's best interests in mind. How could you doubt that? You have no business being on the line mourning her, only to judge every move she made as you saddle up to the woman's coffin. You make me sick!"

The short one shivered as the two women turned toward each other and leaned in with their backs directed at Fiona. "Though, it sure is important for people to mind their own business, don't ya think?"

"Why don't you mind yours?" Fiona shrieked. "How convenient to have friends that judge your every move. I don't know where that woman is going in the afterlife, but there's a special place in Hell for you lot!"

"Let's get out of here," the short one huffed, grabbing her friend by the sleeve of her raincoat.

Fiona followed them with a cold stare as they jumped in their car. The mourners in front of her looked back; some she had recognized. She could see her daughter Rose up near the coffin. Some of the mourners dispersed at the commotion she caused, shortening the line. Fiona nodded at her Rose reverently, offering a polite smile before kneeling in front of the coffin. Fiona could feel Rose's hand on her shoulder as she marveled at her own corpse in the coffin, the fine detail Rose took to ensure the right shade of lipstick was applied to her cold mouth.

“You pay no attention to what these people say,” Fiona said to the corpse. “You did the right thing.”

The slamming of the coffin lid jerked Fiona out of the dream, just as it had the past four consecutive nights.

CHAPTER 5

CARRIAGE HOUSE 4: ASHES TO ASHES

"It's exactly as she said it would be."

Beth O'Brien surveyed the neat row of colorful plaster houses at the lip of the mossy limestone dock of Galway Bay. Her sister Belle walked behind her while Anne, the oldest, fumbled with a duffle bag emblazoned with a Beatles logo out of the back seat.

"Glad you didn't forget Ma," Beth cackled; her wine buzz made each step on the wet cobblestones a challenge.

"Don't drop her," Belle replied. "She'll die if we came this way and she never made it into the water!"

"I won't," snapped Anne. "I didn't have half as much to drink as you did. I'd be dead if I did." She looked around. "This looks just beautiful. Reminds you of Liverpool, doesn't it?"

Beth rolled her head and sighed. "I suppose. Then again, *everything* reminds you of Liverpool and the Beatles."

The women walked cautiously over the uneven cobblestones toward the gigantic rustic boat. The captain turned the bright orange sails so the ship would angle closer to the dock. The first mate's broad chest was squeezed into a tight pair of rubber overalls. His skin had deep creases from the elements, and he wore a weathered baseball cap with salt and pepper strands curling out underneath it. He hopped off and anchored the vessel. He tipped his hat. "Welcome to the Galway Hooker!"

"I resemble that remark!" Beth replied, prompting howls amongst the three sisters and the crew. One by one, they gingerly boarded the boat, which soon sailed past the small lighthouse and the Siamsa, the thatched roof limestone theater where they had attended an Irish step dancing show the night before.

The wind licked the choppy waves, and the crew moved the orange sails around expertly. Belle whipped out her smartphone and took a dozen pictures of the coastline and the boat. Beth might have been the historian of the family, but Belle was definitely its photojournalist. Anne was just along for the ride, offering flinty New England commentary whether she was asked for it or not.

After about twenty minutes in the bay, the captain tapped Beth on the shoulder. "This is a great spot at the perfect time. We're far enough away, and the current has just shifted away from Galway here."

Beth looked at her sisters who were both in tears. She puffed up her cheeks and let the air slowly escape them. "Showtime."

Anne fished out the urn from the Beatles duffle bag. She swept away the curly permed brown hair that blew into her line of sight and then adjusted her glasses. The wind shifted yet again, so she turned her back on her sisters momentarily while she fumbled with the clasp. The captain reverently took the urn from her, tied it into an apparatus at the side of the boat, and lowered the rope toward the water.

"Anyone want to say anything?" Anne asked. "We just gonna lower her into the drink?"

Belle looked over Anne's shoulder.

Anne followed her gaze and spotted Belle adjusting the generous cleavage in her low-cut top that was choking in the confines of the life jacket as she flirted with the first mate. "That didn't take long," Anne grumbled. She cupped her hand around her mouth. "Excuse me!" she shouted. "Would you lovebirds mind breaking it up for a second while we give this good Irishwoman by way of New Hampshire a proper burial? Jesus, Mary, and Joseph!"

Belle's face reddened as she joined her sisters at the other end of the boat. "Killjoy," she mumbled.

Beth nodded. She was a slight woman with long brown hair streaked with blond highlights and olive skin that was a polar opposite to the alabaster complexion of her sisters. She reached into her the pocket of her Chanel trench coat, took out a piece of paper and a pair of leopard print reading glasses and closed her eyes.

"Well, here's to Ma, otherwise known as Mollie Epstein O'Toole. There wasn't a drop of Irish blood in her, and, by all accounts, she married a man with no interest in his Celtic roots. But that didn't stop her from being the most Irish person anyone ever knew. Thanks for instilling a love of this wonderful country in everything you said and did throughout your life and for making us the fine women we are today."

Belle nudged her sister in the ribs. "Are we supposed to bow our heads during this part? Is this a prayer?"

Anne nudged her back. "Is everything a joke to you? Even this? Knock it off!"

Belle tried to suppress a giggle, inadvertently letting out a snort instead, which set off a chain reaction in Beth.

"Mother of God! I have half a mind to dive into the water with Ma!" Anne shouted.

"Well, that would amp up the fun if you did," Beth snapped.

"Come on, sis, lighten up!" Belle shot back. "You know Ma hated the shiva and the seven days of wearing black in her religion. She was a partier! This is exactly how she wanted to go!"

Beth nodded. "Anne, you go next."

Anne approached the side of the boat. "Thanks, Ma, for everything you did for us. Really. I know I didn't always tell you I loved you, even though you wouldn't let up with the affection, but you knew I loved you. Right? I'll see you soon, Ma." She then bowed her head in silent prayer and sniffled.

Belle stepped up ahead of her sisters and looked down. "Well, Ma, this is the end of the road. Thanks for the laughs. Thanks for being my friend even when I didn't really treat you like one when I was a teenager. Thanks for the money you left in the will for that quickie divorce and for making this trip of a lifetime possible. You're a giver until the end, old gal. Love, your favorite daughter. By a long shot." With that, she winked.

The captain nodded and tipped the urn so that the grey ashes made a brief cloud above the water before tucking into the waves.

The three of them stood on the deck, motionless. A seagull shrieked above them, piercing the silence and prompting the women to end their prayers and bless themselves in unison.

The captain waited a minute before approaching them. "Would you like a tour of the Bay? You have another hour left on the boat."

Beth shrugged, batting her eyes. "I could rock away on this boat with you all night long," she replied.

"Oh, Jesus, not this one, too!" Anne protested.

Beth's eyes locked onto the captain's. Her eyes moved from the neat red beard that clung to his tight jaw down to the bulging biceps that strained the thermal shirt under his overalls. Belle's eyes had already moved even lower.

"My name is Colm Burgess. My brother back there is Liam. How long are you girls in Ireland for?" the captain asked gamely.

"We're here for the weekend," Anne replied curtly.

"Well, I'd like to buy yis a drink when we hit the shore, to toast your ma. Where are yis stayin'?"

"Outside of the city, way out," said Belle. A place called Crumlin Manor Lodge or something like that.

"I know the place well. Sure, aren't I going past that place myself on the way home? Happy to collect you and show you a night on the town if you'd like."

"Not much of a town from what I saw on Google Maps," sniffed Anne. "I think we can make it around by ourselves."

Belle batted her eyes. "That sounds divine," she said with a bright smile. "What time do you get off work?"

"I'd say we'd be done here by 7. Have to do some cleaning of the ship. I could be there by 9," Colm said.

Liam called out from the bow of the boat. "My brother isn't going to want to invite his more handsome brother, so I'll leave it up to the ladies. He has all the manners of a sow's ear!"

Beth looked over the captain's shoulder. She hadn't noticed how well the Liam filled out his overalls. Again, Belle had beat her to the punch. "Two for the price of one!" she squeaked. "It's a date."

"I don't think I want to go out tonight," Anne said. "All of a sudden, I'm not feeling well."

"Those are the sea legs kicking your ass, sis," Beth replied impatiently before looking at Belle. "See? We should have left the old one at home. She's slowing us down!"

The men scurried around the deck, tying everything up once the boat approached the dock. Beth and Belle scampered off the boat and looked back to see Anne struggling.

"Jesus, girl! You're 58, not 88!" Belle shouted from the dock.

Anne was swinging her arms like a pitcher. "I'm sick to my stomach, and my joints are starting to get sore," she said weakly.

"You've been carrying around that damned urn since we got here; no wonder your arms are sore," Beth reasoned. "Our work is done here—time to live it up!"

"That's it?" Anne hissed? "Drop the old gal in the drink and go out and party it up? Really? No grieving?"

"We made an agreement that this trip would not be a sad one," Belle shot back. "We've been talking about making this trip over for God knows how long and now that we're here, I have no intention of moping. There's time for that when we get home!"

They rode for the rest of the trip in silence, jostled every now and then by the cobblestones and potholes on the makeshift roads. Belle screeched the tires at the bend of the road as they approached the carriage houses.

"Jesus!" Anne exclaimed in the back seat.

"The guys will be here in half an hour!" Beth said with a panic. "I thought we'd have some time to freshen up, but that damned traffic in the city totally screwed us up!"

"Is that smell of fish from the boat, or are you just getting really excited?" Belle asked.

Beth punched her in the arm. "You dirty bitch!"

"I learned from the best," Belle countered. The sisters in the front seat broke out into fits of giggles.

Anne moaned in the back seat. "Just get me out of this car, please! The way you've been driving in such a rush! I feel like I'm gonna puke!"

Beth jammed the hand break in front of their carriage house. She rushed out of the car with Belle as Anne gingerly attempted to extricate herself from the backseat. She entered the carriage house about a minute after her sisters, who were already arguing about who was going to use the single bathroom first.

"I'm going to bed," Anne called out to her sisters upstairs.

"You haven't had dinner, and it's only 8 o'clock!" Belle shouted over the whir of her hair dryer.

Anne waved at her sisters absent-mindedly. She kicked off her shoes, entered the downstairs bedroom, and shut the door.

Colm had asked that they walk down the driveway a little bit, away from the carriage houses and the prying eyes of the manor owner. The women did as they were told, and, in a few minutes, the lights of his car bathed them on the road.

"Where's your lovely sister?" Liam asked as he craned his neck to see them as they climbed into the backseat.

"Not feeling well, and, besides, you couldn't handle the three of us!" Belle cooed.

The brothers in the front drove the sisters in the back a few miles to Ryan's, a small bar. It wasn't so much a bar as a living room on the first floor of a large home attached to a convenience store and a gas station. As they stepped inside, the jukebox was playing "Dirty Old Town," and the locals were lustily singing to every word.

One of the local women sized the foursome up, rolling a bar straw around her mouth. Beth shot her a dirty look. The reception was considerably warmer as the lads made their way toward the back of the room where their mates were engaged in a spirited game of darts.

"New Hampshire, is that where yeh said ye're from?" asked one sloshed dart thrower.

Belle nodded.

"That's where the presidential campaigns usually start—there and Idaho, right?"

"Iowa, which is near enough I guess!" she exclaimed. "You're really up on the American political process."

"Then is it you we can all blame for that feckin' eejit ye put in the White House this time around? Did ye unleash the monster up there in New Hampshire?"

Belle raised her glass. "Touché! I'll drink to that!"

The shooting pain flung Anne's eyes open wide as she lay in bed. She had soaked the sheets in sweat. The heaviness in her chest was constricting her breaths like a rabbit crushed in the coil of a python. Every muscle was betraying her now, making it a Herculean effort to roll over. Panic swarmed her brain like fire ants on a picnic lunch.

Stay calm. The phone is right over there. You can do this.

Her knees and ankles joined in on the symphony of pain as she attempted to roll onto her side. Her forehead was clammy on the cool pillow.

Get your shit together, girl. This is not the way you're going out. Not here. Not like this.

She clenched her jaw and rolled over again and balanced her frame on her right arm. She dug into the mattress with her elbow and channeled all the strength she had there. With a grunt, she rolled over again, landing in a tight space between the bed and the wall with a dull thud.

"Jesus Christ!" she shouted in between labored breaths. Her forehead and the back of her hands were burning against the baseboard heater, giving her extra adrenaline to wiggle her body away from the wall somewhat. The bed behind her shifted slightly, giving her a little more room to work with. She had to rest and build her strength back up, but she knew time was not on her side. The red dots between the "1" and the "30" on nightstand clock were like silent beacons crying for help that wasn't coming.

"Oh, Jesus! Oh, Goddammit!" she gasped.

Crying out is not going to do anything, she thought. *Save your strength. Get yourself out of this jam you're in and get to the phone. Anything in your mind that's not going to serve that purpose is useless. Get a hold of yourself. Come on.*

She hooked her foot on the frame and pushed onto the legs of the headboard. Success! The waxed wood floor allowed her to slide easily toward the phone. The adrenaline and optimism were like the wind in the sails on the boat had been earlier.

It was short-lived. A new wave of pain radiated in her chest and spread like a ripple through her neck, shoulders, and elbows. It robbed her of her precious breath for ten seconds as she froze in terror.

I'm not going to make it. I told Ma I'd see her soon, and now look! I jinxed myself! How could I have been so stupid? Well, my worst fear was to die old and alone, and now, here I am! New England's idea of Eleanor Rigby, that's me!

"All the lonely people, where do they all come from?" she whispered as she began to lose consciousness.

No husband. No kids. I'm sure Beth's and Belle's kids and their kids will come to send their old Auntie Anne off, only because my sisters will drag them. But who else? I mean, seriously? The old codgers in the Bangor Library, maybe? Would they even miss me?

"Eleanor Rigby, died in the church and was buried along with her name," she whispered.

Who would want kids anyways? I mean, look at the heartache my friends and sisters had raising those ungrateful little shits. The drugs. The rehab. Moving to the back of the line as the main lady in your son's life, right behind the new wife and their new daughter. I see Beth going through some of that now. They'll throw her in a nursing home before long, and she'll die alone, just like me.

"All the lonely people, where do they all come from?" she whispered.

Still, it would be nice for someone to be here holding my hand as I die here. Belle's girl will be there for her. That must be awesome raising a woman who grows to be your best friend. I'll never know that. I was just the mean librarian screeching at the kids to wash their filthy, grubby hands before touching the picture books. Look where it got me? Dying on cold floor in the middle of nowhere all by myself is where it got me. The mean "book bitch" was what Tommy Sanders called me, the fat little bastard.

I guess that's how I'll be remembered. The Book Bitch. Well, kiss my ass, Bangor...over...and...out...

Belle staggered out of the upstairs bedroom of the cottage she shared with her sister and gingerly tottered down the stairs on the balls of her feet.

Beth was already in the kitchen, fumbling with the electric teapot.

"Never again," Belle mumbled.

"That's what you said last weekend and the weekend before that, after the country two-step fiasco, remember?"

Belle started to laugh. "Oh, my God! What's up with your neck? Did he try to choke you last night?"

Beth nodded, parted her lips, and let a sly smile escape her lips. "Oh, he was a wild one. We did it three times. How was the first mate?"

"Not as good," Belle sniffed. "By the time I noticed it was in, it was over!"

The twins laughed, cupping their mouths in unison.

"Shhh! We'll wake up Anne," Belle whispered.

“Well, we’ll have to wake her up anyway. I’ve got to wrap a scarf around my neck to hide the hickeys, paw marks, and God knows what else is there.”

Beth creaked open the door and didn’t see Anne in bed. She reached over the night stand and picked up the scarf. “She’s not in here,” Beth said. “I guess she must have gone over to the main house for breakfast already.”

Belle craned her neck to look into the room as her sister closed the door but not before spotting Anne’s feet on the floor near the bed.

Fiona spotted Beth opening the door of their carriage house. “Oh, here’s yer wan running across the courtyard now. She seems to be in a hurry, maybe trying to make it to confession before it closes?”

“My sister! My sister is dead! Help us, please!” Beth was gulping in air as she spoke, the shock beginning to set in.

Fiona went pale. She darted over to the door and grabbed her guest by the shoulders. “You sit right here. No use going back into that house. We’ll call the ambulance right away.”

Johnny was already on the phone. Belle soon joined them, her eyes and nose puffed red. Within ten minutes, the paramedics arrived. They spent a few minutes in the carriage house before navigating a gurney through the thin doorway as they wheeled Anne’s lifeless and covered body into the back of the ambulance.

"It looks like the poor creature had a heart attack, massive," the paramedic told Johnny as they closed the door. "I'd say she struggled for a few minutes, tops, so thank God it was merciful."

Johnny made a sign of the cross, grim-faced as the man spoke. He held his arm around Beth, whose knees grew rubbery.

"Maybe there was something we could have done to save her, if only we were home!!" she said between sobs.

"It would appear that this took her fairly instantly, missus," the paramedic said, tipping his hat. "I really don't think there was anything you could have done. We're going to take her into the morgue at University Hospital Galway, and we'll await word from you. I'm sorry for your loss."

"My missus is already on the phone with the U.S. Embassy to let them know what happened," Johnny replied. "She has some contacts there, so she's swinging into action."

The emotion was starting to catch up to Beth and Belle and they welled up as the paramedics held hands in a circle, bowed their heads, and prayed before returning to the ambulance. They embraced for a long moment, swaying as they sobbed. Johnny, clearly uncomfortable with the display of emotion, put a reassuring hand on Belle's shoulder before heading to the barn to give the women their space.

Fiona was just getting off the phone. She had a list of questions written down from the Embassy, but that would wait. She outstretched her arms, and both women flocked to her at the same time.

After the two of them composed themselves somewhat, Fiona asked them if they were up to answering some questions about logistics. Beth nodded.

There was no husband.

There was no next of kin and no other living siblings to consult.

There was a will, and Beth was the executor.

There was no burial plot purchased. There was no apparent preference of how her remains were to be handled, but Beth would confirm that momentarily, as she had her laptop and copies of all pertinent documents in her iCloud account to include Anne's will.

Yes, she was a practicing Catholic.

There was a small fortune, under $100,000 U.S., which was all left to the Bangor Public Library.

Fiona nodded as she took notes. She tapped her pencil on the notepad nervously. "Might I suggest something?"

"Of course," Beth replied.

"If there is no burial plot, no clear wishes, and no next of kin to consult on this, we can arrange to have her body shipped back to the States for $10,000 U.S. or you can make a decision right here and now."

Belle cut her off. "To cremate her for a lot less. Brilliant idea."

Beth turned to her. "Oh, my God! Are you serious? We're going to pinch pennies here?"

"Why not?" Belle replied defensively. "If it mattered so much to her how she wanted to be laid to rest, she would have picked herself a headstone, a burial plot, the whole nine yards. She didn't do any of that."

"If I might be so bold, it would be about a third of the price," Fiona offered. "That would mean more money going to the library if that was her intended beneficiary."

Beth wiped her nose with a handkerchief. "I suppose you're right."

Fiona stood up. "Right, so. It's all sorted. I will check with the local church and get everything settled with the morgue. You're welcome to stay here for as long as it takes to settle this, free of charge, of course."

Beth nodded. "That's so sweet of you. Thank you so much, Fiona."

Belle snapped her fingers. "Hold the phone, I have an idea. What if we hire the same charter boat to spread Anne's ashes near Ma?"

"That's a wonderful idea," Beth said between sobs. "I still have Colm's number. I'll call him and let him know what happened.

"Yes, you seemed to make great friends with him and his brother straight away," Fiona replied, biting her bottom lip. "I'd say he owes you one."

The local library league had gotten the word about their fallen comrade from the church grapevine, and they were there, twenty strong, to see Anne off. She was a member of the Rosary Society, and her Irish counterparts were there as well. Based on the interviews he had done with Beth and Belle, the priest spun a short but sweet story about the flinty New England girl who devoured romance novels but never found her Prince Charming. After some lobbying on Fiona's part, the priest reluctantly bent the rules to allow Anne's favorite Beatles song, "Here Comes the Sun," to be played.

The sisters made their second pilgrimage in three days to the docks of Galway Bay. Colm edged his Galway Hooker into port and the women, accompanied by Johnny and Fiona, boarded the ship. When they were about a mile offshore, Beth fished the urn out of Anne's Beatles duffle bag, stopping to study the Beatles logo for a minute.

"You know, if we had given this more thought, we would have spread her ashes on the River Mersey in Liverpool instead of Galway Bay."

Belle considered this for a moment before speaking. "Well, we're here now. I've gotta believe those waterways are connected somehow."

"She really loved her Beatles," Belle replied with a sniffle.

"And Ireland. She loved Ireland, too. But yeah, she loved the Beatles more."

"Keep in mind, the Beatles are all Irish lads," Johnny offered.

Fiona smiled approvingly.

Beth handed the urn over to Colm before turning to Belle. "Remember that song from *The White Album* she used to sing to our kids when she watched them?"

Belle nodded, and with that they began to sing in unison.

Close your eyes and I'll close mine
Good night, sleep tight
Dream sweet dreams for me (Dream sweet).

Colm lowered the urn into the dark, cold water as they sang. Beth and Belle huddled together for comfort and warmth while Fiona and Johnny held hands.

CHAPTER 6

CARRIAGE HOUSE 5: CONFESSIONS

Marjorie threw the car in park in front of the carriage house and lingered in the driver's seat for a long moment.

She stared in horror at her long, bony hands, tracing with the thumb of one hand the ropy veins that pulsated just below the surface of her onion paper skin as she tightly gripped the steering wheel. The endearing freckles of her youth had metastasized into brown puddles of liver spots around her knuckles.

"I have mother's hands now," she cried to no one. She stared at the reflection of her pale green eyes in the rearview mirror, recoiling at the spidery wrinkles that had formed around them.

"You look like your mother, too," she sighed. "Are you 83 or 63? Who knows?"

Her brittle bones creaked as she slowly negotiated her thin frame out of the car. She clicked the key fob and the trunk popped open, revealing a flowery cloth overnight bag that was overstuffed. She grabbed it, gently closed the trunk, and walked toward the main house, fussing with the long silk scarf draped over her narrow shoulders as she walked.

The door opened before she was able to knock.

She offered a warm smile at her old friend. “Fiona,” she said in forced sing-song response as they embraced.

“I’m so sorry for your loss,” Fiona replied, closing her eyes tightly as she dug her chin into her friend’s shoulder.

Marjorie sighed deeply, and her body froze as she inhaled. They broke their embrace, and Fiona followed her friend as she hobbled around the kitchen table.

“Thank you so much for making room at the inn for me,” Marjorie said.

Fiona dismissed this with a wave. “Not at all. Can I offer you anything?”

“A brandy, perhaps?”

Fiona winced. “You have drink coming out of your pores, love. Are you sure that’s a good idea?”

“Tea, then,” Marjorie replied, brushing aside a few strands of white hair that escaped her loose bun.

“You drove like that?”

Marjorie grimaced. “I came for peace, not for judgment. If you’re not up to the task of serving that, I’ll stay somewhere else.”

Fiona nodded deferentially.

Our cross examination relationship hasn’t lost its potency, Marjorie thought to herself.

“I deserved that, I suppose,” Fiona replied. “I’m just worried about my old law school roommate, that’s all.”

Marjorie fixed her gaze at the buttery, oversized leather couch near the fireplace. "I love what you've done here. It's a credit to you, really."

"Have you not seen this already? Weren't you here a few months ago?"

"Was I? I can't remember, to be honest. In the last few weeks, as we reached the end of the line, the days and years seemed to run into one another."

Fiona bit the inside of her cheek and shook her head. "I can't imagine. Weren't you marvelous leaving the practice to be with her during those last few months? I'm sure she appreciated that very much, even if she wasn't able to say it."

Fiona visibly flinched, and her jaw hung open as she witnessed Marjorie burst into tears, howling in anguish as she lowered her head into her cupped hands on the table.

Fiona rushed over and grabbed Marjorie's shoulders. "It's okay, luv. Let it out," she whispered, rubbing Marjorie's back in a circular motion as she convulsed in sobs.

Johnny walked in, saw the scene, and began to walk out. Fiona caught him. "Johnny, would you mind pouring us a couple of mugs of tea? It's going to be a long night."

The long night turned into three days. Marjorie remained cocooned in Carriage House 5, barely moving out of the bed. Fiona would gingerly enter the kitchen every few hours to freshen up the tea service, coaxing Marjorie downstairs with one of her favorite raisin scones. She refused proper dinners despite Fiona's escalating protests.

"There's no talking to you, and there never was any talking to you," Fiona exclaimed, her tone colored with love, concern, and exasperation.

"Yet you keep trying," Marjorie replied weakly as she shuffled from the bedroom to the bathroom.

Fiona's brow furrowed with pent-up worry for her friend.

"Let this play out," Johnny said later that evening, barely looking up from his paper as he sat cross-legged by the turf fire. "The woman's been through murder these last few months, and she is just worn out caring for her mother. That's all that's going on."

Fiona's gaze never left the candle flickering in Marjorie's window across the courtyard. "I've just never seen her like this. She was always the strongest one in law school. She was the rock we all clung to when we were going stark raving mad with the pressure of exams."

Johnny rustled the newspaper and looked over his reading glasses. "I guess it's your turn to return the favor. I've known Marjorie as long as I've known you, and that woman doesn't usually lean on people. She doesn't show people her weakness. In an odd way, I feel honored."

Fiona looked back at him. "Goddamn you for seeing things so clearly sometimes."

Johnny smiled, stood up, rolled the newspaper in a ball, and threw it into the fire. "All in a day's work."

Fiona fished her mobile phone out of her pocket and reached for her bifocals. *You around for dinner tomorrow night? Everything's okay, but it's still a bit of an emergency,* she texted.

The reply came a minute later. "6:30? I'll bring the merlot."

She couldn't decide if it was the grief or her refusal to take in much food that was causing her to get so loopy, but this latest cup of strong coffee had done the trick for Marjorie. It woke her up, gave her clarity, and she was riding it like a wave.

How much longer could she stay here? Fiona and Johnny couldn't have been nicer to her, and of course, she was paying through the nose for the hospitality, but this had to come to an end. They would eventually grow weary of waiting on her hand and foot. They were probably looking forward to seeing the back of her going out the door already.

Her mother's estate was mostly liquid and with assets of her own, money was no object.

There was no going back to that home, she thought to herself, not after everything that had happened there. Where was she going to go next? An only child with no child of her own and with the partner of a lukewarm marriage in the ground a few yards from her mother.

She remembered that time a few months ago when she had heard the schoolchildren walk by her house as she was hanging the wash on the line at the back of the house. One of them told the other that this was the house with the two old, stooped witches living inside it. People rarely saw them outside, the child went on to explain. Some thought they were sisters, one thought they were the mother and daughter, but everyone agreed that there was a giant cauldron that rested on top of a turf fire. The one doing the talking told her younger school chum that her parents always threatened to drop her off at the stooped witches' house if she didn't eat her carrots.

She could still feel the damp wall of the house as she held the basket containing the clot of wet clothes against her hip. She grimaced in the memory of throwing her head back onto the wall and sobbing uncontrollably, loud enough for the children to hear as they scurried down the narrow black top road to the safety of their mammies.

No, she couldn't go back to that town. One witch was buried, and they were all too happy to burn the other one at the stake for all she knew.

The bottoms of her wool slippers scratched the hard wood floor as she shuffled back and forth, her bony arms clasped in a knot behind her back.

What was she going to do next?

She stopped in her tracks. She traced the car as it rolled into the courtyard, and her back stiffened when she saw the familiar figure head into the main house.

"Ah, Jaysis," she said to no one.

Father Quinn sloshed through the puddles that formed in the gravel near the front door of the house.

Fiona squinted to see him through the fog and relentless rain, motioning him into the house. "Thanks for coming," she said, hugging the priest as he entered the house.

He blessed himself. "May the Father's goodness bless everyone in this house."

Johnny nodded.

"You're very welcome Father," she replied before stopping out of the way to allow Johnny to shake the priest's hand.

"What she said," Johnny said with a laugh.

"Still doing the talking for you, I see," Father Quinn chuckled as he tugged on the tight collar that was leaving a indentation on his blotchy neck. "Smart man."

Fiona tousled the man's thinning pale red hair. "There you go again, taking his side. You were roommates before, and you will be again if you keep this up."

"You're looking well, Johnny, fit and trim as ever," Father Quinn said.

"Wish I could say the same," Johnny said, nodding in the direction of his friend's protruding belly.

"Well, it's rude to say no when a parishioner offers you tea and a sandwich after you bless the house, baptize the child, marry the child, baptize the child from the unmarried couple while looking the other way. I could go on."

"Well, there's no talking about a diet tonight," Fiona replied, fussing with the lapel on Father Quinn's black jacket. "You're a sight for sore eyes."

"Where's the patient?" Father Quinn asked.

"She's in Carriage House 5," Fiona replied.

"You wouldn't know her if you walked by her in town," Johnny added.

"I'd know that woman anywhere," Father Quinn replied. "Wasn't she my last chaste kiss before I took my vow of celibacy?"

Fiona blessed herself. "Jesus, Mary, and Joseph!"

Father Quinn looked across the courtyard. "I haven't seen her in years. It's a shame she never really found anyone. You don't think she…"

Fiona cut him off. "Never got over that last, chaste kiss, and you ruined her for the rest of mankind?"

Father Quinn lowered his gaze. "Something like that," he mumbled.

"Don't flatter yourself, m'love," she replied with a giggle. "The law was her husband all those years. We would be in this mad race for who could post the most billable hours for years until I dropped out of the race because of the kids. She kept working at that pace until the last few years, when her mother took a turn for the worse."

Father Quinn shuddered. "The poor thing. Johnny was telling me that over the phone not long ago. I can't imagine being in that small thatch house in a backwoods place like Gweedore with nothing but a demented mother in the cottage with you. That part of Donegal always gave me the creeps with all that talk of the bog faeries and witches we used to hear in school. I don't know how she did it for all those years."

Fiona shrugged her shoulders. "Neither do I. She looks like she aged 15 years over the past few months. Johnny's right. Be prepared for a bit of a shock."

"Will she be joining us for dinner?"

"It doesn't look like it," Fiona replied, eyeing the flickering candle in her window. "Why don't we sit down and have a bite, and if she doesn't come over, I'll make her a plate and bring it over."

The knock on the door never came, so Father Quinn gingerly crossed the courtyard. He pierced the inky blackness of night with the light of his phone, balancing the covered plate in the other hand as he walked. He gently knocked on the door, and after a minute, he heard rustling inside.

Marjorie bowed her head. "Ah, sure Jaysis, are you here to give me the Sacrament of the Sick? I must be in dire straits altogether."

"If I was, why would I bring a plate of food?" he replied with a chuckle. "Why prolong the obvious?"

He always knew how to make her laugh. She resisted the urge to laugh because her mouth had a cud of resentment and regret at the very sight of him. *How long did I pray for this man to come to his senses? Every nun, brother, and priest I know left their orders except for him. What an idiot! Then again, here I am the bigger idiot for waiting on him.*

"The Catholic church seems to be feeding you well," she offered, staring at his bulbous stomach.

There was a forced smile plastered on his face. "You should think about joining the convent. The meals are great, and it looks like you've been missing a few lately."

He put the covered plate down on the small kitchen table to his right. "Fiona and Johnny sent this over. They're a bit worried about you, I don't mind saying."

Marjorie uncovered the dish and inspected it with a frown. She unleashed the utensils from their tight napkin confines and began to gamely pick around the plate.

There was a long, uncomfortable silence between them before Father Quinn made the first move. "I haven't seen or talked to you since your mammy's passing. I'm sorry for your loss. She was always so kind to me."

"Until you left me at the altar for the Lord," she snorted. "That took her a little while to get over."

Father Quinn grimaced and nodded. "Right. I made that one easy for you, didn't I?"

More silence as the tension gathered in her throat like toothpaste through a tube.

"Have you done any interesting ministries lately?"

"A tour through the Vatican was pretty spectacular," he replied, fussing with the cufflinks on his black shirt. "As you can imagine, the church has no shortage of legal issues to sort out, and being a lawyer sure comes in handy."

More silence. Father Quinn shifted in his chair. "Who's saying Mass for you nowadays in Gweedore?"

"I wouldn't know," Marjorie said with a huff. "I haven't been to Holy Communion in thirty years because I feel like a jealous mistress every time I darken the door of a church."

Father Quinn sighed. "So this is how it's going to go."

"What was that?" Marjorie shouted.

"I said, 'didn't you move on with your life?' Didn't you settle down with a nice man and..."

She waved her hand dismissively. "And no wedding ring or children to show for it. Drank his liver away in the pub, leaving me at 31. Some romance!"

"So, that's how it is with you, is it?" he shot back. "I'm the one to blame for everything that went wrong in your life?"

She shrugged. "If you say so."

"Well, that's mighty convenient. It allows you to take no responsibility for how your life turned out, because it's so much easier to blame everyone else. I expected better from you, Marjorie. You were the best, brightest, and the most worldly out of our entire law school class."

Marjorie stood up. "Well, someone obviously slept their way through the compassion classes in the seminary. Is this how you minister to your parishioners? I've seen a million shepherds in my lifetime and none of them got far with their flock by judging and lecturing them."

"You're making it very hard to minister to you."

"I didn't ask for that!" Marjorie shrieked. "Is that what they think over in that main house—poor old widow Marjorie is a charity case? Well, I'll be out of everyone's hair soon enough."

"What's that supposed to mean?"

"You take it however you like," she replied flatly.

He got up to leave. "Clearly, this is a bad idea. No matter what hard feelings you might have for me, I still care for you very deeply, and I am around if you need me: as a priest, as a friend, whatever. God bless you, Marjorie."

She watched him walk toward the door. "Wait. There is something I do need from you."

He turned to face her. "Name it."

"I'd like you to hear my Confession."

He nodded and motioned toward the small kitchen table.

Marjorie blessed herself. "In the name of the Father, Son, and Holy Ghost, amen. Forgive me, Father, it's been 35 years since my last Confession."

"This is going to be a long night," he muttered as he blessed himself, tucking his chin into his breastbone.

"I killed my mother."

His eyes widened. "What did you say?"

"You heard what I said. I killed my mother."

Father Quinn swallowed hard. "How did you do it?"

"With these," Marjorie replied, her gaze lingering on the backs of her hands. "I took the pillow next to her head while she slept and put it over her face. I then leaned in as hard as I could, praying to God the entire time that I wouldn't break her nose or leave any bruise that I had to explain later. The woman had a lot of fight in her, but in the end she barely struggled."

It was Father Quinn that was struggling to find his next breath. "Oh, Marjorie."

She wiped away a tear with the back of her hand. "Wasn't she a week from dying anyway?"

Father Quinn put his elbows on the table and cupped his head in his palms. "Marjorie."

Marjorie's back stiffened, and her eyes darted around the room. She could see her mother's face, her closed eyes and the dark mouth, toothless and sunken. As she held the pillow, she could see her mother's sternum pumping rabbit breaths out into the down pillow that separated them. She held the pillow until the sternum became still. "She was a week or two away from dying, tops. Tops! I'm just after coming down the stairs after throwing my back out from lifting her deadweight to change another soaked nightgown, bed sheet, and diaper. I'm there toweling off after showering the piss off of me, shifting my back to have the hurt meet the hot water compress I've made. I jumped on Facebook for a bit of a break from the madness, and there's yer wan! Just landed in Portugal for a week of hollies! There's herself, jetting off to America to watch her son's conducting debut at Lincoln Center! There's that one, about to walk the gang plank onto that cruise around Australia she's been dreaming about for years. And there I am, cold as hell, a water bottle is all I have for comfort while everyone is living their lives. When I heard her shift in her bed and moan, I..."

More silence.

"What do you want to ask forgiveness for?" he asked robotically.

"That's the thing, Father, I don't know. If this was going to happen in a few days anyway, and I'm the only child, and there's no one else in her life, was there any harm done?"

"I think you know the answer to that," he said, avoiding eye contact. "You said it yourself at the beginning of the Confession: *you* killed *her*. Besides, if your conscience was clear, why do you feel the need for a Confession?"

The room swirled around her. She gripped the table tightly.

"I'd like for you to turn yourself into the police," he continued.

She shook her head, her attention drifting to a picture across the room.

"If you don't, I will," he pressed.

Marjorie's gaze sharpened like a falcon eyeing a distressed baby rabbit. "What does Canon Law say again? 'The very most a priest may do is require the penitent to surrender to authorities and may withhold absolution if the penitent refuses to do so. The Sacramental Seal is inviolable. It is a crime for a confessor in any way to betray a penitent by word or in any other manner or for any reason.' So, given the fact that I am not going to turn myself in, the secret stays in this room."

"I know you can tell yourself that there was no harm done since she was on her way out anyway, but you and I know better."

"This was a mistake," she said with pursed lips.

"And now the horse is out of the barn, so we have to deal with this mistake now," Father Quinn replied nervously.

She nodded slightly, biting the lining on the left side of her mouth. "I have to deal with the mistake, not you."

Father Quinn reached across the table to grab her by the hand. “You’re not in this by yourself. You have myself and the Burkes in that house over there ready to love you and support you.”

Marjorie closed her eyes, savoring his touch once again. *Their hands clasped, arms swinging carelessly as they crossed the Pont de la Tournelle foot bridge in the rain during a romantic weekend in Paris. The first time either one of them had traveled on the dime of a company expense account, and they had been giddy over their good fortune.*

“I don’t want this to ever end,” she had said, looking at the water that rushed underneath the bridge below them.

“It doesn’t have to,” he had replied as his hand fished in his pockets for the small velvet box containing the engagement ring. She had toppled over him as she spun around in shock, and they giggled on the ground as the crowd shuffled around them.

She looked down on her shriveled hand and recoiled, breaking their grip. “Thanks, Father. If you don’t mind, I’m a little worn down right now. Can we take this up in the morning?”

Father Quinn grabbed her hand again and looked at her reassuringly. “That’s grand. We’ll have a nice fry in the morning and get everything sorted out, okay? I’ll be staying tonight in the main house.”

Marjorie smiled and nodded. “We will, so.”

Father Quinn bent over and kissed her hand tenderly before making the sign of the cross at the doorway.

The alarm on her cell phone rang at 3 a.m., but Marjorie was already packed and awake, lying on the bed in her clothes with her eyes wide open. She descended down the stairs, ate the last bit of raisin scone from the night before, and tiptoed out into courtyard. She closed the car door gingerly and released the handbrake, coasting down the hill for a quarter mile before turning the engine at the bottom of the hill.

The headlights of her car pierced the predawn darkness, and the nettles and tall grass that peered out of the stone walls slapped the side of the car as she swerved across the narrow road.

She convulsed with heaving sobs as she drove. *That bastard had called the shots all of their lives, in his presence or absence in her life, she thought to herself. He wasn't going to say how it goes again! He was right in one respect: she had spent way too long blaming him for how her life had turned out.*

"I'm behind the wheel now," she cried out defiantly, shaking her fist as the car careened on the slick road.

Where was she driving? Where could she go to feel home? It was a mystery to her until the headlights illuminated the N17 road sign. It was muscle motion that drove the car through Donegal and over to Gweedore. The dawn light waged battle with the curtains of fog that formed in the valley of town as she sped past the church, her eyes blinking through the redness, rawness, and heartbreak.

She got to her mother's house, hopped out of the car, and slammed the door.

"The witch bitch is back," she yelled, chasing it with a throaty laugh. A small, emaciated orange cat crept toward her, mewing frantically, scolding her owner for abandoning her.

"You look like absolute hell," Marjorie said, looking down. "Join the club!" She tottered into the house and tied her red scarf on the front doorknob as the cat kept close to her. She looked nervously around the kitchen, locating the stockpile of cat food cans in the cupboard that her mother kept for any of the many stray cats that prowled her fields. She and her mother took a liking to this little one, who slithered through her legs as she walked.

Marjorie looked down at the cat. "How great it must be to be a cat. No one has any expectations of you. No husband! No one telling you to move on after the drunk you picked as your husband drinks himself to death! No worries of a church stealing the love of your life! No ties to your mother. She has a litter, licks and nurtures you for a few weeks, then shoves you away. 'Fuck off and fend for yourself,' your mother says! No attachments from there! Seems like heaven to have a mom like that and a life like that, except for the fleas below and the hawks above, I suppose."

She fumbled with the can, which hissed open when she pulled the tab, and dropped the food on the floor.

"There you go, now, pet," she said. "Glad that made your day. Probably saved your life today, based on how those ribs are showing on you. Maybe I'm good for something. You still need me, don't you kitty?"

She paused, looking down at the cat before looking up at the heavens. "Well, this is sad. A mangy stray cat is the only thing on this earth that cares if I come home," Marjorie bellowed, startling the cat away from her pile of food. "Jesus, I've become one of those old crazy cat ladies after all that education, all that hard work, all those lives supposedly saved in the trials I've been part of! This is it! Nothing to show for it!"

She then moved to the kitchen table, grabbing one of the old chairs and placing it in front of the open front door. The breeze rustled through the musty house, catching one of the white drapes. It startled Marjorie, who thought it was her mother's ghost. She looked up, hurled the other end of the tied scarf over the door, fished out the cell phone in her purse, and dialed.

“Hello. Yes, I’d like to report a murder of my mother,” she said. There was a long pause before she spoke again. “She’s already buried…”

She stood up on the chair and tied the other end of the scarf tightly around her neck before continuing.

“Yes, yes, I’m still here. What’s that again? Yes, I did it. You can find me on the bend right off the Gweedore crossroads, first house on the right…yes, the white one…yes, thank you.”

She closed her eyes at the moment and thought of *Thelma & Louise*: the power and the guts it took for the pair of them to drive off the cliff at the end of the movie. They told the world to eat their dust. She opened her eyes and blessed herself before jumping off the chair.

She could feel her neck crack as her back hit the front door hard, knocking the remaining breath out of her body. Her legs flailed, kicking the door and the chair as she swung from the doorknob.

Don’t fight this, she thought to herself, attempting to beat back the licks of panic that engulfed her. She followed the blue light on the dashboard of the police cruiser as it sped up the hill toward her house. It was the last thing she saw before going limp against the door.

Marjorie heard the beeps first and then became aware of how dry lips were. She tried to lick them but she couldn't; her tongue was pinned under the breathing tube that was jammed down her throat. She moved her head to the right before her eyes fluttered open. There was a doctor leaning over her, grabbing the sides of her neck with his thumbs and her gaze followed the gleaming stethoscope around his neck as she attempted to focus her mind.

"The bruises are healing, and there is minimal damage to her trachea, thank God," the doctor reported. "Looks like your friend is going to pull through."

Marjorie attempted to turn her head but flinched as the pain stabbed her below the ear. She heard footsteps walk around the bed and watched as Fiona plopped into the leather chair by the bed. Father Quinn came around the bed as well, draping his hand around the chair as he leaned in.

"Thank God she's awake," he said, blessing himself. "It's okay, dear. You're safe here now."

The doctor asked if the rehabilitation arrangements were made, and Fiona nodded, her wilting gaze never breaking away from Marjorie's face.

Father Quinn fidgeted with his pocket watch. "I'd best be heading off soon; people find out there's a priest on the floor, and I'll be pulled into every room for a blessing."

That's Quinn for you, Marjorie thought. *Always running out the door at the slightest sign of awkwardness. Some shepherd of faithful he turned out to be!*

Father Quinn bent down and planted a loving kiss on Fiona's cheek. She closed her eyes and nodded, clearly savoring the affection of her old friend. Fiona watched the priest walk out of the room and waited for the door to close before she leaned in.

"You gave us quite a scare, Marjorie," she uttered through a clenched jaw. "I never saw a man pray so hard in my life, priest or otherwise. He still loves you, you know."

Marjorie blinked, and her head nodded slightly.

"We sat here and prayed together for what seemed like hours, and at some point, I started to divert the intentions of those rosary decades away from you and on to me. I mean, why waste a Hail Mary?"

Marjorie intensified her stare.

"Jesus, Mary, and Joseph! While some of us are trying to hang on to our lives for as long as possible, there you are, giving up the will to live. It's hard to muster up prayers or sympathy for the likes of you. What's that, you say? 'I just lost my mom, give me a break?' Yeah, well, I buried my parents, too; it's hard, and then you move on. You go through the first set of holidays without your mammy, and then your life becomes the new normal. That ache dulls, and you just adjust to it. But there is a different kind of ache that never goes away once you know you don't have much time left. You ache to watch your son walk his new wife down the aisle. You ache for more time to grow old together with your husband. You ache to hold your first grandchild. That is real heartache, my dear." Fiona turned her body, calculating each twist of a muscle as she attempted to stand up. She sighed as she walked over to the bed and leaned into Marjorie. "I would give anything for the time you tried to piss away," Fiona hissed before balling her fists and spinning around toward the door. "I'm done praying for you, Marjorie. Time for you to pray for me. Pray for me."

CHAPTER 7

CARRIAGE HOUSE 6: DESIGNER DISASTER

Shari Taubman pushed the ostentatious designer sunglasses to the top of her head once she emerged from the cab. She spun around, closed her eyes, and caught a lungful of the cool, sweet air.

This is about as far away from New York as you can get, she thought. *It's perfect.*

Based on the paparazzi she had to avoid at Shannon Airport, it might not have been far enough away. The world was fascinated by this disgraced Manhattan socialite and public relations maven who manipulated social media for her clients only to find herself a victim of online shaming.

Her descent started in United's President's Club Lounge at Vail Airport; the gaggle of partying girls she was traveling with as part of her sister's bridal party were snacking on champagne and marijuana-infused chocolate cordials when a tipsy French businessman approached the group. He made some cheesy attempt to hit on one of them, prompting a series of catty comments amongst the women that were so hilarious in Shari's inebriated state that she felt the need to instantly share.

Thanks/no thanks to the Pepé Le Pew smelly French guy with bottle-opener teeth who just tried to hit on us. This is the best romantic France can do? #limplovers

It was the tweet read around the world. In the time it took to power down her phone once the airplane cabin door closed to when the plane landed in LaGuardia, the French Embassy had retweeted the country's displeasure, the Renault car company had fired her PR agency, and countless French nationalists were rooting for her downfall on Twitter in a series of snarky tweets while she was in midair. *#ShariTaubmanIsToast* was the trending hashtag of the day on multiple social media platforms.

Flight pattern shows this uptight bitch is up over Chicago now, blissfully unaware that her world is crumbling down below.

#ShariGrubmanIsToast needs a can opener for that bug up her ass she has about French people. Sacre bléu.

Hope someone gets a picture of her pathetic Botoxed expression when she lands and finds out she has been shit-canned. #karma #ShariTaubmanIsToast

We are agog! We are aghast! Is Shari Taubman ruined at last? #LeMizReference

"Vous êtes viré !" which translates into "you're fired" in French, would be the headline that hung over her glamour shot in the Paris newspapers the following morning as they gleefully announced her dismissal from the international firm she had founded. The national news outlets would couch this story as a cautionary tale of viral shaming in this electronic age, and the local New York rags kept the story alive for weeks by interviewing every client of the fired employee who still had an axe to grind against her.

The cows in the field looked completely disinterested in this fallen celebrity in their midst as she grabbed the collar of her butter yellow bomber jacket and lugged her luggage in front of the carriage house. One of the maids answered the door, greeted Shari in broken Polish, and ushered her into the kitchen. Fiona was circling the table on her cell phone, smiled at Shari, held up her pointer finger, and attempted to conclude her phone call.

"Right, so. Yes, she just came in and is standing in front of me now. Yes, thank you for the heads-up. Right, so. Bye."

Shari smiled. "Fiona?"

"And you must be Shari. We've had a few people ask if you were staying here already, and it's not even 10 in the morning yet."

"Sorry," she said sheepishly. "Welcome to my life. I really need to hide out."

"Might be a bit difficult with that long blond hair. I'm afraid not many people wear it quite like that around here..." Fiona struggled to find the right words.

"Wear it as long and loud as I do?" Shari grinned. "You can say it."

Fiona smiled. "Yes, well, there might be wisdom in wearing it under a ball cap or something."

"Or I could cut it. Or color it. Or cut and color it. Do you know anyone?"

"I do of course," Fiona pronounced with a nod. "She even makes house calls."

"Perfect!" Let's wash the platinum life out of my hair once and for all! This new year is all about change in attitude."

Fiona reached for her phone on the table and made a brief text. "I just texted my friend Anne Marie. She's trustworthy, very discreet, and right around the corner."

Fiona's phone buzzed, and she looked down. "She asked if she can come over before her kids get home from school at half three. Will that suit you?"

Shari nodded enthusiastically. "My God. You're a lifesaver! If she can come in the next hour, that would be amazing!"

Fiona texted and got an instant response. "You're all set. Do you need help with the bags?"

"Just the ones under my eyes," came the reply. "If you don't mind, I'm going to nap for a half hour before I gotta do my new 'do."

I like this one, Fiona thought as she watched Shari cross the courtyard to her room.

Shari started to cry when she saw the new brunette bob haircut.

"Ah, Jaysis, I feel terrible," Anne Marie stammered. She was a stylish woman in her early forties with a pale complexion and bright eyes that now dimmed with worry. "You don't like it."

"No, it's fine. It's great, actually," Shari uttered between sniffles. She grabbed Anne Marie's hand to reassure her. "It's just that I haven't had a brunette bob since my bat mitzvah."

"Since your what, dear?" Fiona asked, leaning in.

"Bat mitzvah. Like your Confirmation."

"Oh, right," Anne Marie and Fiona replied in unison. The erupted in giggles.

Shari couldn't stop staring. She gently tapped her taut cheeks. *This is who I am, she thought. This. Brunette. Let this Botox crap get out of my system. Get back to the real me.*

Fiona put her hand on Shari's shoulder and put a grocery bag in her lap. "Here. This is a Galway football jersey that belongs my daughter, and you appear to be about the same size. The lads in town just won the All-Ireland final over the weekend and everyone and their mother will have one of these on over the next few weeks. If you really want to blend in, put this on."

Shari rested her head on Fiona's hand as it rested on her shoulder. "This means more to me than you know. I always heard that Irish hospitality was the best in the world, and now I know why."

"We're a lot friendlier than the feckin' French. And sexier, too, if you don't mind me saying," Anne Marie squeaked.

The women broke into fits of laughter.

Fiona's disguise worked like a charm. She spent the morning in the shops around Tuam, shucking the designer sweat suits that were her trademark in favor of the more sedate fashion of this western European country outpost. Exhausted from jet lag, she dropped her bags, pulled the brim of her Galway baseball cap low, and sunk into a comfortable chair in the Correlea Court Hotel in the center of town. The government-owned media company presenter sat at the news desk announcing to the country that Shari Taubman was rumored to be hiding in the west of Ireland, and she watched with a sense of satisfaction as a pair of male paparazzi sent there to cover her sat at the bar and gripe to anyone who would listen about how Shari eluded their grasp.

What would I tell a client in this position? she thought. *Own the mistake. Look contrite. Quit your job. Change the narrative as soon as possible.*

The narrative of the presenter changed at that moment as breaking news about a terrorist bombing by The Louvre Museum in the center of Paris blared across the bar.

"Jaysis, those feckin' Al-Qaeda savages are at it again," one bar patron, looking up at the screen, remarked to his wife as she sat at the barstool next to him. "I'll tell yeh, Europe is going to hell in a hand basket."

Shari looked down, adjusting the leg on her yoga pants as the journalists walked by her. When they left, she fished the small iPad out of her purse and began typing a statement.

Johnny collected her in town, and the silence between them was punctuated only by the occasional comment about the greenery or the rainy weather. Shari smiled at him before hopping out of the car and heading into the main house. The women at the table straightened their backs as she walked in. Shari began to back out of the house, but Fiona waved her in.

"You're fine, not a bother, we're just finishing up the meeting. These are my friends, Edith, Jane, Philomena, or Phil for short, and Grace."

The women nodded at one another. Based on the measured body language, Shari could tell they had been talking about her.

"Our last meeting," Phil sighed. "I still can't believe the government denied us funding."

"On what?" Shari asked. "Back in the States, I did a lot of pro bono fundraising and PR work."

Grace's tongue made a lump on the side of her cheek. "Right. Well, Not sure you're going to be able to help us in this country," she replied curtly.

Fiona threw her a dirty look. "That was rude! Never mind her. We can use all the help we can get." Fiona slid a pile of papers toward Shari. "Our whole sad story is in there," she continued. "There is a local train station no longer in use here in Ballyglunin. It was one of the locations where they shot *The Quiet Man*, starring John Wayne and Maureen O'Hara. Have you ever heard of it?"

"No," Shari said, taking her iPhone and a pair of electric-pink readers out of her pocket. "But that's why God invented search engines!" After a few clicks, Shari looked up.

"So, the search shows that this movie is in the top five all-time favorite movies, according to IrishCentral.com. I also see that there are more than 46 million people claiming Irish heritage in the United States. What have you been doing to reach them for funding?"

Fiona raised her eyebrows and stared at Grace. "See? She might be useful after all!"

"I'm not seeing anything in the search engines about the railway station," Shari continued, never looking up from her device. "I can organize a Facebook and Instagram landing page for that, and if I were you, I would spend a few hundred on advertising there and have the analytics target your likely donors."

"Jaysis, is it English she's speakin'?" Phil asked. "That whole thing went right over this old lady's head!"

"Mine as well, but she certainly sounds like she knows what she's doing," Fiona added before turning to Shari. "Unfortunately, we cannot pay for your services."

Shari laughed. "I don't know if you've noticed, but I'm not terribly busy at the moment now that the whole world hates me. Happy to do it for free; it might help change the conversation globally if I am seen as a do-gooder instead of a spoiled brat. I'll get right to work on it." She pushed out her chair, smiled, and left the women at the table.

"Jaysis, don't get in her way," Phil said.

Grace turned to Fiona. "Do you really think it's a good idea to be associated with her? The things they've been saying about her in the news!"

Fiona carefully considered this for a moment, tapping her legal pad with a pencil. "I'm not condoning what she's doing; she just seems like a lost kid now, and one careless, drunken mistake might ruin the rest of her life. It's a pity."

Grace looked down, stirring her tea. "I don't like her. She's a pushy New Yorker."

"Maybe pushy is what we need," Phil asserted. "If the Irish government won't help us fund the repairs, the rest of the world might!"

The one lane road that ran around the farm made a perfect jogging path, Shari thought as she leaned against her carriage house to stretch her back leg muscles. A light rain had just passed over Ballyglunin, leaving droplets to hang on the branches like glistening jewels. She began her trot around the farm, taking in the sights of white lambs prancing in the meadow and of a flock of large black crows hopping after a baby rabbit in the short grass. As the path took her toward the front gate of the estate, she noticed a silver Volkswagen Golf on the side of the road. She halted and plucked the earbuds out of her head as she caught a glimpse of the long camera lens jutting out of the crack in the car window.

"Shit! The jig is up!" she screamed before galloping back to the main house. She was breathing heavy when she burst through the door of the main house.

Fiona leapt from her chair. "Everything all right, dear?"

"No, the paparazzi is at the bottom of the hill," Shari exclaimed between gasps. "Why don't they leave me alone? I have to get out of here. It's not safe."

Fiona grabbed her by the arm. "Get a hold of yourself. You can't run forever! What would you tell a client in this position? I read online how many PR nightmares you've navigated others through; it seems the longer you avoid the story, the more legs it takes on."

Shari was shaking. "I know, I know, I know! You're right. I always tell them to own their mistakes, take their lumps, and change the narrative as quickly as possible."

Fiona winked. "Now, we're getting somewhere. Well, you already took your lumps by losing your job and being hunted and jeered at by everyone online. Let's go to work on the other parts, shall we? I have some ideas."

There was a gaggle of television crews and cameras in front of the limestone and steel gates that lined the entrance of Crumlin Manor House. Fiona and Shari strode proudly down the driveway, hands clasped, and the cameras whirred to life as they approached the gates.

"Thank you for coming," Fiona announced. "I am Fiona Burke, friend and legal counsel for Ms. Shari Taubman. We're happy to take questions."

The reporters shouted over one another, and Shari answered everyone in even tones.

Yes, she was sorry for her comments.

Yes, she was learning from her mistakes. Lesson learned, among others, was not to mix champagne and edible marijuana before logging into a social media account.

Shari was taking that hard-learned lesson and forming Mulligan House, a haven for people trying to regain their name online after a misstep. A "mulligan" was a golf term for an extra shot you can take following a poor one.

Shari was also helping the locals on a global campaign to raise funds for the Ballyglunin Railway Project, to save the train station and Irish cultural landmark from dilapidation.

With that announcement, attention turned to Fiona.

"Are you concerned that the campaign to save the train station might be tainted by your association with Ms. Taubman?" shouted one reporter.

"Not at all," Fiona replied. "I am not condoning what she said. Look, she made a mistake, but as they say in the Colossians, 'Forgive as the Lord forgave you.' She is sorry, and she has certainly paid a high price. To forgive someone and to encourage that person to do better with a second chance is in compliance with Christ's teachings."

“Are you worried about the impact on your law firm for taking on a client like Shari Taubman?” shouted another reporter.

“I am representing Shari, not the law firm,” she replied. “I left the firm a number of months ago and am now happily retired from the rat race.”

“What would you say to the French people as you stand by the woman who said such mean things about them?” asked another reporter.

“France and Britain declared war on Germany during World War II, less than a century ago,” Fiona countered. “Now, the German Chancellor is the leader of the European Union along with France, and it is Britain that is threatening their union with Brexit. France has shown a nice ability to not dwell on things and adapt to the present, and I'm quite sure the French people will eventually come around in this case as well.”

Shari blinked, opened her mouth, and jerked her head back. “Well, *that* was a brilliant assessment of the world. Fiona Burke for President of Ireland!”

The next morning's news cycle was plastered with images of Shari on the jogging path and then facing down reporters with Fiona at her slide. Coverage was mostly favorable, with the occasional editorial wagging its influential finger at Shari to do better next time. On the following day, there was no mention of her. The press had gotten their story and moved on to another one and with it, Shari enjoyed the first restful night sleep in weeks.

Grace was still reluctant to accept any help from Shari, but the rest of the Ballyglunin Railway Restoration Committee seated at Fiona's breakfast table could barely contain their glee. There were more than 10,000 likes on their Facebook page with another 40,000 fans on Twitter. Both outlets encouraged fans to give at least a Euro to the cause, and overnight, the committee sat on €100,000 that they didn't have the night before. When Shari entered the kitchen, all but Grace gave her a standing ovation.

"We cannot thank you enough for what you've done for us," Phil gushed.

"Please. The debt is entirely on my shoulders. You stood by me when I needed a friend the most, and I will never be able to repay you."

Her eyes turned to Fiona who nodded once and met her gaze with a warm smile. "I guess there is one thing you can do to repay us," she said. "We are looking to organize a benefit concert over the next few weeks to raise more money. Do you think you can stick around to help us with that? We have nothing to offer you, but you can have the carriage house rent-free if you'd like."

Shari nodded. "The price is right. You have yourself a deal!"

Phil grabbed the end of the table and slowly rose from the table. "I'll be on my way now. The grandkids are coming over because my Owen just got one of those Shetland ponies for the front yard. After raising ten kids and kicking them all out, I need a feckin' mouth to feed in my house again like I need another hole in the head."

Everyone laughed as they got up from the table. Fiona grabbed Grace's arm gently. "Can you hang back for a moment, luv? I might need your help with something."

"Of course," came the reply. The women hugged one another and soon it was Grace and Fiona alone in the kitchen.

"Tea?" Fiona offered as she poured steaming water into her mug.

"I'm stuffed, thanks," Grace countered, the hesitancy evident in her voice. She took off her horn-rimmed glasses, blew on the lenses, and wiped them with her scarf.

"I'm going to ask you if you were the one that tipped the press off that Shari was here," Fiona said, her eyes locked onto Grace's.

"Absolutely not! What would make you say something like that?"

"A hunch. A hunch I'll apologize for if I am wrong."

Grace crossed her arms. "Well, I'll take that apology now."

Fiona had studied witnesses for too long to be fooled by Grace's flimsy defensive posture. "You're one of my closest friends, but lately it seems like you're coming to the door with more and more judgments. Adnan and your opinion that he squandered money on the cell phone. Shari being a pushy Yank. You see where I'm going with this?"

"I think so, and I don't like it," Grace hissed.

"Well, I don't like it either," Fiona snapped. "Having you blow in and out with the wind gossiping to the neighbors about this one and that one is not only hard to be around, it is bad for my business. If you can't leave the opinions at the gate, maybe you should think about driving past the house."

"I've never been so insulted in all my life!" Grace shouted as she got up and headed toward the door.

"This year of hosting others has taught me that everyone has a story, everyone has a struggle, and, most of the time, that struggle is something that doesn't bubble to the surface. Jaysis, don't I know that myself."

"This is all your fault!" Grace screeched at Shari, who was getting ready for a jog in the courtyard. Grace popped the clutch, reversed, and sped down the driveway.

Shari looked toward Fiona with a puzzled look.

"I think we found our leak in the bucket," Fiona said with a wink. "She'll get over herself, and if she doesn't, good riddance to her."

CHAPTER 8

A BRAVE DAD

Upper West Side of Manhattan, September 2013

The cab jerked to a stop in front of B'nai Shabbos, an upscale Jewish temple on 86th Street in Upper Manhattan. Maura Kelleher grabbed her purse, fumbled with some spare change to settle the $30 cab fare, and reached for insulated bag that was next to her in the back seat.

Though her lithe 74-year-old frame was well sculpted by tai chi and yoga three times each week at the local YMCA, her bones creaked today with dread underneath her heavy overcoat as she navigated out of the car. She tightened the elaborate silk Book of Kells print scarf around her head to ward off the whipping March wind that chilled Manhattan on this brilliant sunny day. Her thick transition lenses began to darken in the light of the sun as she walked a few steps into the synagogue.

She had been praying daily to live to see the day that she would become a grandmother, and as of last week, she discovered the Lord had answered her prayers. Her only son, Sean, broke the news to her that a one-night stand with a Jewish girl from Keane's Bar on McClean Avenue in Yonkers had produced a son, and the shock that her prayers had been answered gave way to sheer joy at the sight of him in the hospital. That joy was gone as she stood on the steps of the synagogue and contemplated the impossible: her first and only grandson was to be raised Jewish and ushered into that faith with a bris ceremony.

She made her way into the ornamental banquet hall inside the temple, shaking her head at the irony that the room was lit by Waterford Crystal chandeliers from her deceased husband's hometown. As soon as she looked down, the guests began to approach her.

"Yes…L'chaim to you as well…yes…howya…yes, I'm the grandmother…thanks, thanks, yes, L'chaim to you as well." Her eyes locked onto Sean's, who offered a weak and embarrassed smile. She gave him the once over, shaking her head in disgust, what with the rumpled shirt begging for mercy as it stretched over his distended belly and the clip-on tie that hung beneath his watermelon bald head.

Sean's large frame was in perpetual motion as beads of sweat gathered on the forehead of his round face. He bent down to give his mother the briefest of kisses.

Maura looked around before leaning into her son. "Howaya, Sean," she whispered. "Why is everyone walking up saying 'L'chaim?' What does that mean in Jewish: 'She could've kept her legs closed?'"

"Ma! That's a prayer!" Sean hissed.

Maura blessed herself. "Jesus, Mary, and Joseph, I'm sorry. I'm just a bag of nerves. Where do I put these?" She unzipped the contents of the insulated bag and produced a Pyrex dish neatly sealed in tinfoil. Sean looked down, shaking his head.

"Ma! You brought pigs in a blanket—to a bris? Really? Did you forget what this is?"

"How can I forget?" she shot back. "I've been up all night in bits about this so-called bris, trying to figure out how I'm going to make small talk with a room full of strangers while they hack up my first and only grandchild in the corner!"

Sean rolled his eyes. "Ma, this is a bris. It's religious. Very spiritual. The rabbi is a professional."

"You know who else is a spiritual, religious professional as well? A priest!"

Sean shook his head. His blood pressure began to rise and a pink color began to form across his face as a result. "Ma, we've been over this! Rachel is Jewish, and that means Ryan is Jewish at birth!"

"Yeah, well. Of course, if you were married to the woman, you might have more of a say in how the child would be reared..."

Sean cut her off. "Not this again. You're never happy! After all the Rosaries praying to the Blessed Mother to make you a grandmother before you die, I finally came through."

Maura gazed at the ceiling in mock prayer. "You've got quite the sense of humor, my Lord and Savior Jesus Christ! You had to wait until my feckin' son grows into the age of a grandfather himself before you answer my prayers!

"This is nothing more than divine intervention, Ma!"

Maura fretted with lint on her teal wool overcoat, avoiding eye contact with her son. "Yeah, right. I'm still getting over the shock, but I don't know why. The way you prowl around the bars night after night with yer arm around this one and that one. You're not fooling me! I've got eyes in the back of my head!"

"No, you've got eyes on Facebook all day is what you have. That's it, Ma, I'm unfriending you."

Maura was horrified. "You wouldn't dare!"

Sean fished his cell phone out of his pocket and swiped on the glass. “Yeah? Well, I just did. You know, I’d really appreciate it if you just laid off, Ma. Rachel’s been through a lot, never mind me.”

Maura was outraged. “Her! How about your poor graying mother! You spring it on me just a fortnight ago that there was a baby, now I have to watch your new ‘family’ slice his poor little unmentionables! I tell ya, I don’t know how much more of this I can take!”

“There you go again, making it about you,” Sean exclaimed through gritted teeth, the color in his face reddening. “What about me, huh? You don’t think this is a whirlwind for me? I thought I’d glide into my golden years carefree. Now, I’m going to be paying college with my Social Security checks!”

Maura threw back her head and cackled. “Well, you didn’t get that thing down there between your legs for stirring your tea! Sure, I’ve been saying that for years until I’m blue in the face, a lot of good that did us! Now we’re here in this position, you and I, sonny boy! Sitting here helpless while this crowd does who-knows-what to him when we both know what this boy needs is a proper Baptism!”

“Ma, a little tolerance? It’s Jewish custom!”

Maura started to sniffle. “No mention of Catholic custom…no Baptism…no christening gown…no bonnet…no wiping of original sin from the soul. Some Jewish butcher hunched over my precious angel. Ah! I’m getting dizzy!”

Sean laughed. “And the winner for Best Actress in a series...”

Maura cut him off. “Laugh all you want! No grandson of mine is going to Hell!”

“He’s not going to Hell! Give it a rest, willya? I’m not saying no to a christening. We just have to wait until I can negotiate visitation rights.”

Maura crossed her arms and bit the inside of her cheek. "Negotiate visitation rights? Is that how it goes nowadays with the young ones, the ones who sleep with whomever you want without thinking of the consequences? You sound like a prisoner with your talk of visitation rights. Well, then again, you do the crime, now you do the time, my love."

"Funny. Really funny," Sean retorted. "I'm going to ask to take him on the weekends once he starts breastfeeding a bit. That will give me time to set up a christening maybe. Until then, I gotta worry about assembling all the baby crap I got in the gift registry."

Maura froze in terror. "What gift registry?" she asked.

"I set one up online, Sean stammered. "You know, for all the stuff I'd need in the apartment. The relatives from Ireland were so great. They couldn't do enough for ya, I'll tell you."

Maura hung her head low. "Jesus, Mary, and Joseph…you told the relatives at home?"

"Y-y-yeah…you mean, you didn't? I sent them an email for the gift registry at Target. What's wrong with that?"

Maura felt pure hot rage welling up inside her. "What's wrong with that? Ah, sure Jaysis. I can just hear my sister Fiona now, cawing like magpies on a telephone wire back home, spreading the news that old Sean got a young wan up the pole, like!"

"Aunt Fiona is not like that, Ma," Sean countered dismissively. She couldn't have been nicer when we spoke over the weekend and said we were welcome to visit the manor any time we wanted to." Sean pressed on. "You forget that the Blessed Mary was Jewish, also pregnant out of wedlock. If it was good enough for Jesus, it's good enough for my son."

Maura pressed her bottom lip with her tongue and shook her head. "You're no Joseph the Carpenter, sonny boy," she said with a snort, looking over at Rachel as she spoke. "And look at the way that one over there is dressed! The tight black skirt and the fishnets! She's more like Mary Magdalene than the Mary the Blessed Mother if you catch my drift.

"Again, no winning with you. If we aborted it, there would have been hell to pay."

Maura blessed herself. "God forbid! Ah, my little man. He's so gorgeous, like."

"He sure is," Sean replied, beaming with pride.

"Can you imagine all the poor innocent and beautiful babies like him yanked out of their mothers' wombs by a coat hanger in a back alley? 'Tis why I chain myself to a Planned Parenthood fence once a month. We must fight the good fight for the little ones!"

Sean shoved his palm in his mother's direction to stop the conversation. "I'm not going to get into the argument about Planned Parenthood and how they actually help prevent more pregnancies with their work. But whatever. Look, I don't like this any more than you do. I can't even look at what the mohel is about to do, circumcising the baby in front of all these people, but let's just get through this, and we can talk all you want later, okay? Just behave now!"

With every ounce of strength she had, Maura offered a forced and icy smile to the rabbi who nodded at her as he walked by.

Sean nervously grabbed the withered old man with the craggy white beard into a bear hug. "I'm the dad!" he exclaimed.

The rabbi nodded. "With a name like Sean and that goyish punim, am I to assume the mother is Jewish?"

Sean wiped his sweaty, meaty palms against his pants. “Yes, she’s over there.”

“Well, let’s just hope for the little fella that the mohel’s bedside manner is better than that when he goes snipping,” Maura offered.

The Jewish congregation scattered to the corners of the room, creating a clear pathway for the rabbi to reach the baby. As soon as he passed, the crowd gathered around the dining room table, their backs turned to Sean and Maura.

“Baruch Haba,” they all said in unison, startling the pair of them. After mumbling something to themselves for a few minutes, a tiny, anguished howl from the lungs of the infant pierced the room. This was immediately followed by a loud crash in the back. The crowd turned to face Maura, who was crouched over a passed-out Sean. As the crowd rushed in to help, two old women in the front slipped and fell on the pigs in the blanket that were strewn across the floor.

Ballyglunin, County Galway October 2017

Johnny parted the curtains watching intently as his sister-in-law’s rental car pulled into the carriage houses.

“The Wicked Witch of the West has arrived,” he sighed.

Fiona stood behind him. “How do I look?”

“For the tenth time this morning, you look grand!” He was lying, and she probably knew it. There had been subtle changes the past few weeks that he had been cataloging. Gone was the ruddy complexion in her cheeks in which blush would be wasted. Her increasingly paler skin was beginning to accentuate the decades of tea stains on her teeth enamel. The suit she was wearing fit her perfectly, only after the tailor had taken it in substantially just earlier this week. He knew her sister's arrival had her on edge for the past two weeks, but the time had come, sooner rather than later, to address these changes with her.

Johnny went out to the car and matched the strength of Sean's iron handshake. He then engaged in the awkward choreography of a hug with Maura before peering into the backseat to marvel at the cute little boy asleep in a child seat. He fumbled with the keys of Carriage House 7 and let Sean in to transfer little Ryan into the bed. Maura's gaze was fixed at the majestic main house with awe for a brief moment before a sudden shower of rain breached the nearby mountains and tumbled into their valley.

Fiona threw open the door and greeted her sister with a hug. Maura held onto her for a moment longer than normal. "You're very welcome back home," she sang.

"The place looks absolutely marvelous," Maura replied, doing her best to swallow her jealousy. "It's a credit to you and Johnny, really. It looks like something out of a magazine in here!"

"I picked up ideas here and there along the way. Johnny falls asleep early, which leaves me time to binge-watch as many home improvement shows as I like! By the time he wakes up, he has a to-do list a mile long!"

Maura inspected her little sister for a moment. "You've gone terribly gaunt, and you look tired, even in the few weeks since I saw you at Colin's wedding. Is everything okay?"

Fiona nodded. "I suppose it's all beginning to catch up to me," she replied with a sigh. "Leaving my job. Taking on the house and this new innkeeping business. The trip over and back to London and then to America over the last few weeks. We're not getting any younger, you know!"

"I pray that's all it is, luv. Still, you look sick, Fiona. Have you been checked by a doctor lately?"

Fiona turned her back and headed to the sink. "I've got tea on the range. You must be knackered from the trip."

Mercifully, the squeal of little Ryan broke the tension for Fiona.

"Nana! I saw cows outside! There must be hundreds of them!"

Maura stooped down to meet her adoring grandson's gaze. "Really? We'll have to go check them out! I heard Auntie Fiona and Uncle Johnny have been so busy around here that she hasn't had the chance to name them, so maybe we can help them out."

"Did you know the ones with the horns are called bulls, Nana! They're man cows. Uncle Johnny says you should never turn your back on a bull!"

Maura tousled the boy's hair. "Uncle Johnny is a smart man."

Fiona embraced Sean. "Fatherhood suits you, Sean."

"I'm glad to hear you say that! I gotta tell you, I'm hanging on by a thread. This is a young man's game."

"Well, you should've thought of that before you rolled the dice," Maura replied icily.

"Yeah, well, if I wasn't in the presence of Auntie Fiona."

Ryan cut them off, grabbing his father's hand. "Uncle Johnny said there is a big rooster here, Daddy! Can we go see him? Pleeeeeeeaaaseee?"

Fiona reached for the bucket of slop and crumbs from the morning's breakfast on the side of the wood stove and handed it to Sean. "You drop some of that in front of the rooster, and you'll have a best friend in no time!"

Ryan squealed with delight and bolted out of the kitchen. Johnny's eyebrows raised in concern as Sean darted after his son. "Ryan! What did I tell you about running out ahead of your dad like that! You're just asking for trouble!"

Maura shook her head and turned to her sister. "It's not normal for a 55-year-old man to be running after a 4-year-old son like that, is it? He's cruising for a stroke, I tell ya!"

"Isn't Mick Jagger just after having a baby and, sure, he's as old as Methuselah's cat!"

"My Sean is a far cry from Mick Jagger," Maura scoffed. "I'm telling you, I've worn out the Rosaries praying for the pair of them."

Fiona looked out the window adoringly. "Well, I suppose the prayers paid off. They look as happy as larks, the pair of them! Sean was always a big kid!"

"That's the problem! All he wants to do is play with him! The boy needs a father, and sometimes you have to ask yourself if Ryan is the more mature one of the two of them!"

The blood started to drum in Fiona's ear canal as her blood pressure rose. "Can the man do anything right?" she said through a clenched jaw.

"Excuse me?"

"You heard me," Fiona replied, turning to face her sister. "First you say he's too old to be a dad, and then when he exhibits youthful energy, you chastise him for being a big kid. Is there any winning with you?"

Maura sniffed. "Whose side are you on?"

"I'm on the family side," Fiona replied evenly. "Where does this get you? I mean, really? Yeah, the guy made a mistake.

Don't you think he knows that by now? He got someone up the pole. So what? He's out there in my backyard doing the right thing and making the best of it! Look at him out there playing with the little dote of a boy! How many men nowadays do their deed and never see the woman or child ever again? You didn't raise a man like that."

"You're damned right I didn't," Maura sniffed reluctantly. "It's just terrible, the way they exist. Sean only gets him every other weekend and then a night or two here and there when 'she needs a break,' as she says. A break? Can you imagine? I hardly ever get to see him. You should have seen the hoops I had to jump through to get him out of the country without her."

"Did you ever think to yourself, 'gee, maybe if I'm a bit nicer to her, I wouldn't have to jump through hoops at all?' Did that ever occur to you?"

Maura swatted her away. "I've been nothing but nice! She's the one that started in with the cold shoulder from the minute I met her! Uppity Jewish bitch from the Upper West Side of Manhattan thinks she's too good to talk to the likes of me. Well, to hell with her!"

Fiona bit her bottom lip as her eyes danced. "Well, okay then!" she exclaimed with a chuckle. "That definitely comes across as nothing but nice. I'm sure she's feeling the love from all these miles away."

"Never mind that. I need your help with something."

"Name it," Fiona said absentmindedly, staring out the window at the young boy as she spoke.

"Now that I have him here, I was thinking of having him baptized," Maura said flatly.

Fiona turned to face Maura. "He wasn't baptized yet? Why?"

"The mother forbids it. It was fine to make a big show out of snipping his unmentionables in front of a rabbi, but God forbid we put a christening gown on him! It's shameful! Anyway, we have him here now, and she won't be any of the wiser. Can we get him over to the parish priest this weekend?"

Fiona looked at her in disbelief, shaking her head. "I don't think that will be allowed without the parents' consent. Is she forbidding it from happening? Because if that's the case, I don't think it's a wise idea to go against the mother's wishes on this."

"Oh, come on! We're talking about the child's soul here!" Maura cried, her voice lilted in desperation.

"Get a hold of yourself and think this through, will you? Let's say you do this thing in secret. Don't you think little Ryan will just run to his mother, all excited about the visit to church? She will catch wind of this, and then what will that do to your relationship? You think you have troubles gaining access to him now? Ha! Wait until this happens!"

Maura bent her head, catching it with the palms of her hands. "What am I going to do? The child's soul is still stained with original sin! I am up at night in bits worrying about that. What if something happens to him?"

Johnny walked out of the barn toward Sean and Ryan, his arm behind his back to conceal a brown paper bag wrapped tightly with packing tape. "I found this among some old things and thought you might like to have it."

After he tore at the paper, Sean paused to wipe a tear from his eye. "My County Galway jersey! I remember this! You kept it all these years?"

Johnny nodded in the direction of Ryan. "I bet you were his age when you wore it. I bet it would fit him nicely now. Wanna try it on him?"

Sean bent down, took off Ryan's shirt, and replaced it with the dark maroon, white, and yellow jersey of the Galway football team. "This is so great. I can't thank you enough!" He motioned to Ryan. "Stand up against that stone wall for a minute and let me get your picture."

Ryan did as he was told, posing as his father snapped pictures on his mobile phone. The boy lit up with delight as the rooster turned the corner of the barn, followed by a few hens. "Dad, we need more slop!" he exclaimed, running after them. The birds scattered at his feet.

Sean looked down on his phone to edit the pictures he had just taken before uploading them to Facebook.

While he had taken his eye off of Ryan, the bull in the field could not stop staring at the colors of the football jersey. As Ryan climbed through the wide bars of the fence and tumbled clumsily into the field to chase the rooster, the bull exhaled loudly and began tapping on a submerged cobblestone.

Johnny called out loudly to Ryan from the opposite end of the bar, snapping Sean out of his fascination with social media. The bull was trotting toward the boy now, who was paralyzed with fear. A stream of urine ran down his leg as the bull charged toward him.

Sean fumbled with the latch of the gate and started the wave his hands and scream at the bull as he ran, but it was no use: the animal was locked on his target. With two large lunges, Sean was able to grab Ryan and twist away from the bull just in time. The bull crashed into the gate instead of them; Sean could feel hot breath on his forearm as a ton of muscle whizzed by him. The bull regained his composure in a few seconds and ran after Sean, who was reaching for the gate. The bull lowered his body and placed his forehead at the back of Sean's knees. He jerked his head, launching Sean and Ryan into the air and over the fence. Sean drew Ryan into his chest, twisted, and landed on one foot, There was a loud crack of bones before Sean fell onto his back, never losing his grip on Ryan. The pain caused him to black out just as Maura and Fiona ran out of the house. Ryan started to cry from the shock, loosening himself from the dead weight of his father's arms before running for the comfort of his grandmother's embrace.

The ambulance sped up the driveway within minutes. In the meantime, Johnny had taped Sean's mangled leg against a board to keep it from moving and disinfected the wound with whiskey while he writhed in agony in a mud pile.

"Is my daddy going to be okay?" Ryan asked, standing behind his grandmother as the paramedics maneuvered Sean into the gurney.

"He will be," Maura replied. "You're going to stay here for a few minutes with Auntie Fiona while I take Daddy to the doctor to make him all better. Will you be a good little man for me while I'm away?"

Ryan nodded.

Maura bent down to kiss his cheek, and as she straightened her back, Fiona grabbed her gently by the elbow. "Sean saved that little boy's life," she whispered. "That should tell you all you need to know about how good of a father he is." Fiona then kissed her sister lightly on the cheek before briefly embracing her.

Ryan blew kisses and ran after the ambulance for a minute before racing back to the house.

“I hate it when she’s right,” Maura mumbled as she entered the ambulance.

“Jesus, did shock absorbers ever make their way over to Ireland?” Sean cried out, grimacing as each pothole rattled his injury.

Maura grabbed her son’s hand. “They’re doing the best they can. These bog roads weren’t made to carry vehicles this size.”

“Well it’s 2018, for Chrissakes!”

Maura bowed her head, fumbling for words. “I probably don’t say this enough, but that was a really brave thing you did back there, throwing yourself in harm’s way to save your son like that. I’m very proud of you.”

Sean stared at his mother, allowing the moment to sink in. “Wow.”

The ambulance jostled again.

“Ow! Motherfucker!” he screamed.

“Language!” Maura shouted.

“You try being calm with a bone sticking out of your leg!”

Maura looked at Sean’s feet. “Motherfucker,” she sighed.

The ambulance erupted with laughter.

Sean reached for his mother’s hand. “Thanks, Ma.”

CHAPTER 9

CARRIAGE HOUSE 8: AN OLD FLAME

Hannah Shanley fussed with the fringes of the frilly tablecloth, looking into the milky tan abyss of hot tea in her mug. She gritted her teeth as her father paced in the kitchen.

"I won't allow this," he shouted. You tell Fiona Burke you're not coming to work. She should know better than to ask you for a job.

"I asked her," she stammered, avoiding the gaze of her father. She nervously tucked the strands of strawberry blond hair behind her large ears as he walked around her. "She didn't ask me."

"Why would you do a thing like that?" Jack Shanley was a short stocky terrier of a man, with wiry white hair running wild along his eyebrows and jutting out of his ears. He smoothed down the thin strips of hair that stretched across his shiny head and formed a bridge between his two sideburns.

Hannah looked over at the twisted figure in the corner for moral support, but her mother only offered a blank stare. Her osteoporosis had bent her into a permanent L shape, and the third successive mini-stroke a few weeks ago had reduced her communication to a mumble.

"Don't look at her; there are no answers there," Jack bellowed.

Hannah's knuckles whitened as she gripped the side of the table. In an instant, she sprang up and came within an inch of her father's face, startling the old man. "All of the answers are there," Hannah screeched, pointing at her mother. "I've got a 15-year-old car with 600 miles on it because I'm not able to drive! Himself won't allow it! One of the two drivers in the house is paralyzed, and that leaves himself who doesn't want to go anywhere! What's going to happen to me when you go as well? Did you ever think of that?"

"I think of that a lot," he shouted. "I let you out of my sight for one moment, and there you are, flirting with some strange Yank looking for a good time with one of the local girls at my bar. God knows how you'll carry on when I'm dead and gone!"

Hannah rolled her eyes. "Jaysis, are you going to throw that in my face? That was over 25 years ago, Daddy! I've been imprisoned in this feckin' house ever since!"

Jack swung the back of his hand, slapping Hannah in the face.

She sprung backward, gripping the sink for support.

"I'm not going anywhere and neither are you!" he said.

Hannah grazed her swollen lip with the back of her hand, inspecting it for blood. She fixed an icy stare at her father with green eyes, grabbed her purse on the counter near the wall phone, and turned her back on her parents. "I might not be able to drive, but I can walk, and I am walking out of here."

"You walk out of this house, and you can forget about coming back."

Hannah stopped in her tracks, turning her head without looking at her father. "You'll change your tune by about 6 I suppose, after Mam has her fourth or fifth diaper change. I'll see you then."

The rush of emotion and the adjustment of her eyes to the brightness outside made her dizzy for a moment. She steadied herself. For the first time in her 54 years, Hannah Shanley was flush with confidence and freedom. She nodded to assure herself, tugged at the dowdy cardigan that clung to her slender shoulders, and took the first step forward in her sensible ballet flats. She cautiously walked up the steep hill to the crossroads and made a right toward Fiona Burke's estate. As her walk became more animated, her long ponytail swept her bony back.

I should have done this years ago, she thought to herself as the pantyhose enveloping her thighs swished underneath her sensible blue skirt. *What was I thinking, letting the car rot in the driveway outside the house and my soul rot inside the house for all those years? You can blame that old fool all you like, but I'm the fool. I'm the one who pathetically clung to his pant leg when he decided to move away from New Jersey and back to Ireland 30 years ago. What was I thinking?*

The morning dew hung on the leaves above and on the moss that had grown on the limestone walls lining both sides of the road. The cows grazing in the field next to her house lazily made their way toward the wall, chewing their cud as they walked.

"No corn for you today, ladies, sorry," she cried out. After walking about a mile, she rounded the corner toward

Fiona's house just as a car screeched behind her, coming to a stop just inches from the back of her legs. She jumped in a reflex, losing her breath at the sudden motion.

"Sorry, sorry, the teenager's voice said from the passenger window as they slowly drove by. "Dad is new to this driving at the opposite side of the road thing. The teen waved as they sped by, and Hannah gamely waved back. She watched as the right blinker signaled a turn into Fiona's house.

"Well, here we are, in one piece," Dennis O'Dowd announced proudly as the car came to a stop in front of the carriage houses.

"You almost made that woman road kill back there, you realize that?" replied Jane, who was forcefully pressing the glass on her smartphone. "Please tell me there's Wifi in this place. Cell service sucks!"

"Yeah, well, welcome to Ireland," came the sarcastic comeback. "Remember, it was your idea to bring us here."

"Hello? I wasn't going to miss Grandma's funeral!" she retorted.

"Watch your tone," he replied. "You might have had to come here. I did not."

Jane's demeanor softened underneath the "pink pussy" knit hat she defiantly wore everywhere. She grabbed her dad by the shoulder.

"Sorry, I was just frustrated. It really does mean a lot you're here. I couldn't face this without you."

Dennis wove his fingers into his daughter's, nodding. "I wouldn't let you do this alone, my love."

His knees creaked as he negotiated his broad-shouldered frame sideways out of the tiny rental car. A cold wind brushed his bald head, which had an increasingly thin crown of reddish gray hair around the ears. He was terribly self-conscious of the baldness and covered it up with a tan tweed hat that had become his trademark. He clicked the key fob and the flimsy trunk door came to life, revealing their two small suitcases.

Fiona appeared in the open door of the main house. "You're very welcome," she said, wiping her hands with a tea towel before extending it to Dennis. He shook her hand, meeting her eye briefly before looking around.

"Thanks, I'm Dennis, and this is my daughter, Jane," he said. "This is a beautiful place. What purpose did these buildings serve back in the day?"

"Some were horse stables, some were sheds for the turf, hay, or wool storage," Fiona replied proudly. "We spent about three years renovating them, one by one. It's been a labor of love."

"Certainly, it looks that way," Dennis replied. He gently kicked the side of Jane's fashionable boot to get her focus off her mobile phone. Fiona smiled and gave a knowing nod in his direction.

"I'd say you're probably knackered from the flying and the driving," she said. "You're in Carriage House 8, right over there. I can have my husband help you with your bags."

Jane waved her away. "We're fine, thank you. Do you have Wifi here?"

Fiona chuckled. "My kids would die without it. Details are in the card on top of the kitchen table in your flat. C-R-U-M-L-I-N, all capitals, with an exclamation point at the end. There's an electric teapot and some scones on the table as well, and there's a full Irish breakfast inside if you'd like."

Jane looked at her dad. He nodded. "I think we'll take a rain check on the breakfast. Jane didn't sleep on the plane." His daughter grabbed both suitcases out of the car and tottered toward the door.

Dennis stood for a moment in the courtyard, inhaling huge gulp of the fresh air. "That smell of the turf, there's nothing like it."

"You've been here before, I assume?"

"I have, back in the day," he answered. "My wife's family is from the other side of Tuam. We would come to visit her parents. We're here for her mother's funeral."

"I'm sorry for your loss," Fiona replied, bowing her head. "And your wife?"

"It's complicated," Dennis replied, letting the air escape beneath his bushy red mustache that was speckled with gray. "We had just finalized our divorce, then she got in a car accident about a year ago, and now she's living with me and Janey again."

"Sorry, I didn't mean to pry," Fiona responded apologetically.

Dennis nodded. "No harm done. You had no way of knowing. My wife is too banged up to come to her mother's funeral, and I didn't want to have my daughter go it alone on this one, so here I am!"

Fiona looked over his shoulder, her eyes focused on Hannah as she walked up the driveway. "Well, if you won't be having the breakfast in the house, I'll see you to your room. I have a new bookkeeper starting today, and that will give me time to get things settled.

Dennis followed her gaze, turning around to watch Hannah walk. He squinted. "Well, she had an eventful start to the day, I can tell you that," he said with a laugh. "That's the lady we almost slammed into on her way into the driveway. Please let her know that I'm sorry about that."

"Not a bother. She seems to be walking just fine."

Dennis headed toward Carriage House 8 as Hannah walked down the driveway to meet Hannah. "Why didn't you ring me on my mobile like we discussed? I would have picked you up."

"I needed the exercise and wanted to clear my head," Hannah replied. "I've been a bag of nerves all night."

Fiona gave her a hug. "You'll be fine. We're delighted to have you, and we are desperate for the help around here! But first, let's get a cup of tea in you!"

Hannah entered the room first, and Fiona looked at her from behind, shaking her head in disbelief. She was dressed in sensible blue flats, a skirt, and a plain white blouse, which peered out of the holes of her homemade crocheted cardigan. *She looks 74, not 54*, Fiona thought.

Hannah had been an exotic curiosity of the parish for years, with the townspeople speculating about how the poor old girl was able to carve out a life for herself after being under Jack Shanley's thumb for so long. Their privacy made the Shanley home life stuff of much gossip, elevating their only child to this mythical status. A sighting in the supermarket was akin to spotting a unicorn, and when Fiona ran into Hannah at the Supermac two weeks ago, she somehow worked up the nerve to ask her to work for her. Now she could scarcely believe her eyes as Hannah paced her kitchen.

"This is one of the most beautiful houses I've ever seen," Hannah gushed. Her speech was dotted with occasional hard Yank accents, the "ever" sounding like "evaaaah."

"Thanks," she said. "Please sit down and have a cup of tea."

"Are you sure?" Hannah was tentative. "I know I'm on the clock now."

Fiona let out a laugh. "Well, I'm the boss around here, and I say we have tea. We have all the time in the world to hit the computer and find our way around the bookkeeping software."

Hannah's body tensed. "The books are done on a computer?"

"Yes, dear. Is that okay?"

Hannah burst out crying. "I'm afraid this isn't going to work. I haven't kept up on the new technology lately and…"

Fiona grabbed her hand and looked her in the eye. "It's okay! I'm fine with you taking the time to learn. I heard you were the top accountant in your class when you lived in New Jersey; I'm sure that kind of thing comes back to you soon enough."

"But you could get a young kid in here with no problem, and he'd be up to speed in a minute."

Fiona cut her off again. "Like I said, I am the boss around here. If I want to invest in you, that's my worry, isn't it? We've got plenty of other things to do around here while you come up to speed, so I have no worry of you earning a proper wage if you're willing to be flexible with me."

Hannah wiped her snotty face and tears with the sleeve of her cardigan. "Thanks, missus, I appreciate it. More than you know."

"Knock off the 'missus' talk. It's Fiona. Bring your tea with you, and we'll head up to the office."

The women crossed the courtyard to the tall steeple in the corner. They entered the small door next to Carriage House 8 and made their way up the stairs to the loft above the carriage house. The steeple had numerous windows on all sides, providing a breathtaking view of the fog licking the tops of the green mountains of Abbeyknockmoy. In the gaps between the windows were customized bookshelves bent to match the circular room; the shelves were lined with books and family photos.

"How do you get any work done looking at this view all day?" Hannah asked.

Fiona fired up the large screen of the iMac on the corner desk. "I have an old version of QuickBooks. I know there are tons of upgrades and tricks I can get, but I'm not trying to balance the Bank of Ireland's budget here; I just want something simple to navigate through."

She spent an hour with Hannah, who caught on quickly. Still, Fiona found herself shaking her head in disbelief as she stood behind her, shocked at how little she knew about email and computers. They heard the door close in the carriage house down below.

"The American family down there is on their way to a wake," Fiona said, heading toward the stairs. "I'm going to check on them to see if they have everything they need."

"Grand," Hannah replied, deep in concentration as she entered figures into the QuickBooks log.

"A pub attached to a funeral parlor. Leave it to the Irish to come up with the greatest combination ever!" Dennis exclaimed.

The gravel crunched under their feet as they walked through the crowded parking lot of O'Malley's. They had barely entered the dimly lit structure when Jane immediately darted to the open arms of her aunt, leaving Dennis by himself. He stood tentatively in the back of the room, watching Jane.

God knows what poison his wife put into this well, he thought. The squabbling over the unpredictable shift work of a fireman. The lack of inclination to get a second job like the other firemen did to take advantage of the early retirement and to make ends meet. The lack of inclination on her part to get any job at all once Jane went to school. Based on the forced faces on the relatives that once greeted him so warmly, it was a safe bet that many of the details of their rotting marriage had made their way over to County Galway by letters, hushed phone calls, and now emails.

Someone put a gentle hand on his shoulder from behind. "Thanks for coming," Ailish whispered. She was the wife's first cousin.

"You could be shot for saying that," Dennis whispered from the side of his mouth.

"Ah, feck the rest of them. There's two sides to every story, and I'm sure our Marie was no angel, either. It was good of you to come and support Jane, and I think you're a saint to allow Marie to live in the house until she gets back on her feet. You've divorced fair and square; you didn't have to do that."

Dennis looked down on his feet, the emotion welling inside of him. "Thanks for saying that," he replied softly.

She tugged his shoulder again before making her way back into the crowd.

Dennis eyed his former father-in-law, who dutifully stood by his wife's casket. Dennis thought the man did everything in his power to avoid eye contact with him, which was nothing new. Mickey Spillane had grand plans for his daughter that didn't include marrying what he called the "drunk Yank chasing the fire," so the men had little use for one another. Dennis slithered through the crowd toward the coffin, knelt in front of the closed casket for a brief moment, hastily made the sign of the cross on his chest, and made his way toward Mickey. "I'm sorry for your loss, Mickey," he said, shaking his hand.

Mickey nodded. "Thanks. It's good to have Jane here. Thanks for bringing her."

Dennis nodded. "No problem."

There was a large, awkward silence between the men that seemed to last forever.

Mickey's daughter Adele, a painfully thin woman obsessed with running marathons, swooped in and slapped Dennis on the back. "There he is," she exclaimed. "Looks like you're not missing too many meals over in the States. You should come out with me and have an ol' jog around the hills."

"Hello to you as well," Dennis retorted, leaning in for a clumsy hug and kiss. He looked over his shoulder and saw the line piling up waiting to greet Mickey.

"I'll be out of your way now. I'll head over to the pub next door."

"There's a shock," Mickey uttered under his breath for everyone to hear.

Waves of torrential rain slammed the gravel parking lot as Dennis hopped over the puddles toward the pub. It was a small room with dated paneling and a matching bench that covered three of the walls. A few sets of low, round tables with stools were placed in front of the bench, and a large bar made of the same wood paneling stood in the middle of it all. A man went outside when his mobile phone rang, and Dennis took his seat at the bar.

The bartender nodded in his direction and Dennis called for a Guinness. He started pouring the pint, pausing to let it settle, "Are you with the wake next door?"

"I am," Dennis replied. "Grace Spillane is the mother of my ex-wife."

"You don't sound like you're from around here," he replied.

"I'm from the States. New Jersey."

"Sure, everyone's from New Jersey," the bartender said with a laugh, slapping the edge of the bar. "I spent some time over there tending bar for a while at my uncle's bar in Bayonne."

"Get out! I lived in Bayonne for a while! What was the name of the bar?"

"Shanley's," he replied. "On 26th and Broadway. Ever been there?"

Dennis's head fell limp onto his chest. "I cannot believe this. Are you kidding me? I spent I don't know how many nights in that place! It wasn't the same after your Uncle Jack sold it. Whatever became of him?"

The bartender reached for a few pint glasses on the bar and began dipping them into the sink of hot water. "Old Jack is still kicking, but God knows for how long. He lives on the bend of the road near the old Crumlin school near that Ballyglunin Post Office. Been there ever since he moved back from America."

"Wow. Freaky coincidence! I'm staying in that area, though I don't think he'd appreciate me running into him.

I made a play for his daughter once—Hannah, her name was—and he flew into a rage at me. Some people say he moved back to keep me away from her!"

The bartender laughed. "That sounds like my Uncle Jack all right. He's fiercely protective of his wife and Hannah. The locals nicknamed the family 'Herman's Hermits' because they mostly stick to themselves, tucked at the base of the small bridge on the bend in the road."

Dennis leaned back on the barstool, which creaked under his weight. "So, Hannah never married?"

The bartender shook his head. "That cousin of mine has never been kissed, as far as any of us can tell. I haven't seen much of them in a good few years, so I can't be sure."

Mourners began to fill the bar, which signaled the end of the prayer service. A pair of women were chatting loudly behind him. "Came all this way and couldn't even bother to get his arse off a barstool to say an auld prayer for his daughter's grandmother," hissed one of them.

Dennis swallowed his pint in a few gulps and put a 10 Euro note on the bar. He spotted Jane chatting with his cousins in the corner. "That's my cue to leave," he muttered, grabbing his raincoat.

Dennis's mind raced between having to concentrate on the narrow and dark road, the trickle of family observations that Janey offered in the passenger seat and his memories of Hannah Shanley.

He remembered that time, right after he had proposed to Cara, when he spotted Hannah doing the bookkeeping at the corner of the bar. She was pure light, and he laughed at how the innocent flirting between them flushed a fresh supply of blood to her pale skin every time they blushed.

This was before the age of cell phones that tracked every move, so it was easy to slip out at lunch from the firehouse to meet at the bar. She would be there, balancing the books and hopping off the barstool to help her parents when the crowd started to overwhelm them. He fell in love with her naiveté, a trait not shared by her father.

"Is my burger that good that you feel the need to come back every day?" he had said, a raptor's gaze at the ready to measure Dennis's response. He threw his head to the side in the direction of Hannah, who was perched on the stool nearby. "I hope so, because that's all that's on the menu here, if you catch my drift."

The lunches mushroomed into prolonged coffee breaks, where he would escort her a few blocks to the bank so that she could make the day's deposit. He would sometimes pick her up at the corner in the car, and after a quick trip to the bank, they'd snake their way through a few blocks to the Hudson River waterfront to get the best view of Manhattan. The one awkward kiss they shared was bursting with a passion he had never felt with his fiancée.

"My father will kill me," he recalled her saying as she pulled away from his embrace, her face flush with lust.

"That's something I could give two shits about," he had replied dreamily.

She straightened up in her seat. "Well, you should. My mother and father are the world to me and come with the package, just to be clear. They'll be asking about me, so we better turn the car around and head back."

They had said nothing on the way back to the bar. That was a Friday; he was greeted by new owners of the bar that Monday and had gotten the news that the family had moved to Ireland in the middle of the night. It later came out that old Jack Shanley had begun to put feelers out on the bar right about the time Dennis began taking his lunch hour there and that when the bar sold, he had begun negotiating a lease with an option to buy on his house. Both deals had closed on that Friday afternoon.

Hannah had been on his mind these last few months as he began measuring the factors that led to his painful divorce. Was the lack of passion for Cara that had come to light in the kiss with Hannah the sign of a doomed romance? Why did he seek companionship with Hannah immediately after putting a ring on Cara's finger?

"Dad!" Jane shouted, yanking him from the backward glance. "I think you just missed the driveway to our hotel!"

Dennis made a turn into the next driveway and headed into the right driveway. Jane hopped out of the car when they parked, her phone screen lighting her face as her boyfriend's FaceTime call came in. She rushed toward the room ahead of her father, no doubt eager to put distance between them for privacy. Dennis eyed the main house and saw the light on in the kitchen, so he knocked on the heavy door. Fiona looked through the window at first before opening the door.

"You're very welcome! Can I fix you a cup of tea? Or would you like something stronger after the wake?"

"A beer if you have it, thank you," he replied. "I'm not intruding, am I?"

"Not at all. I just drove my bookkeeper home after reviewing our accounts, so please excuse the mess. Fiona hastily scooped up the folders of receipts from the table as she spoke. “How did everything go for you this evening? I mean, as well as it can go under the circumstances.”

Dennis winked, made a gun with his fingers, and pulled the trigger in her direction. “Bingo. ‘Under the circumstances’ is the operative part of that sentence.”

Fiona frowned sympathetically. “That could not have been comfortable for you. I know teenage daughters don’t appreciate gestures like that, but I do. Let me know if I can do anything for you.”

Dennis arched his bushy red eyebrow. “Actually, there is something you can do for me. Do you know a woman by the name of Hannah Shanley?”

Fiona let out a laugh. “You’re joking, right? Hannah is my bookkeeper! This is her mess on my table!”

“The lady I almost hit with my car yesterday is Hannah Shanley?”

Fiona nodded enthusiastically. “The very one! Why do you ask?”

“We knew each other when she lived in America. We had something going, but her father plucked her from me in the middle of the night.”

Fiona nodded and smiled broadly. “That sounds like her father, all right. You know, she never married.”

Dennis winked. “There is a legend back in America about the Irish matchmaker. Am I looking at one of them right now?”

Fiona giggled. “I’m just stating a fact. Of course, if you did want any assistance.”

“Get out while you can,” Johnny said as he came down the stairs. “My wife is stirring up trouble; I can feel it from upstairs.”

Fiona swatted the air in front of her with a tea towel. “Pay no attention to him.”

Dennis stood up and shook hands with Johnny, and they exchanged introductions. "I'm afraid I opened up the can of worms your wife is holding in her hand right now," Dennis said to Johnny, slapping him on the back gently. "Let me get through the burial tomorrow, and we'll see where we go from there. Is she working here tomorrow, by chance?"

Johnny rolled his eyes. "Ah, sure Jesus, here we go."

Fiona scowled at her husband playfully for a brief moment before turning her gaze to Dennis. "As a matter of fact, she is!"

There was furious knocking at the front door that startled the three of them. Johnny jumped up and raced toward the noise, flinging the door open. Jane was in the doorway, wide-eyed and scanning the room for her father.

"Dad! I just got a call from Aunt Rosy. Mom took a fall down the stairs in your house and was rushed to the hospital!"

Dennis went pale. "Ah, Jesus. Is she okay?"

"I don't know," Jane replied, blubbering and sobbing between words. "Aunt Rose said we should take the next plane ride home!"

Dennis put his head in his hands. "I don't know how much more of this I can take, I'll tell ya."

Fiona had already reached for her iPad. "I can check the airline sites to see what the availability of flights are back to Newark for tomorrow. Johnny's sister is a travel agent, and I can have her work her magic to switch your flights to tomorrow if there's room on the plane. Don't worry about the extra night in this room. I can go online and cancel that for you."

"I'll run back to the room and get our reservation information," Dennis replied, wrapping his arm around his shaking daughter as they scurried out of the house.

The fog made a swirling gray carpet that hovered over the grass as they loaded their bags into the trunk of the car, just as the sunrise scaled the other side of the mountain range in the distance. Fiona stood at full attention, fully dressed, with a bag of scones and two Styrofoam cups of tea in her hand. “Take these for the road,” she said, handing the bag and cups to Jane, who nodded her head appreciatively.

“Thanks for everything. You have a lovely home!”

Dennis leaned in and put his arm around Fiona’s shoulder before pulling an envelope out of his blazer pocket. “Would you make sure your bookkeeper gets this?”

Fiona looked up at him. “I will indeed. It’s such a pity you missed one another.”

“Story of my life,” he replied, shrugging his shoulders. “Thanks for everything you’ve done for us, Fiona. Please thank Johnny as well.”

They climbed into the small Volkswagen hatchback and backed out of the parking spot before following the thin trail out to the main road.

Fiona paced the floorboards of her kitchen, offering Jack a tight smile as he dropped Hannah off at the front door. Jack refused to make eye contact as he sped out of the horseshoe driveway. Hannah wiped her feet on the mat before coming in, much to the annoyance of Fiona.

“Never mind that, get in here quick!” she hissed.

Hannah's eyes widened. "Everything all right, ma'am? I'm not late, am I?"

Fiona let out a laugh. "Not at all, not at all. One of the guests who stayed here last night left you a note."

"For me?"

Fiona nodded. "His name was Dennis O'Dowd. Said he knew you from the old days in New Jersey?"

Hannah steadied herself at the kitchen table, looking down at the sealed envelope. "Jesus! Dennis was here? Was he here looking for me?"

"Well, not exactly," Fiona replied. "He was here with his daughter escorting her to the funeral of her grandmother at the other side of Tuam. He's divorced from the wife and all, but she had an accident and couldn't make the trip over. She had another one while they were over here, and the two of them took off like a shot back to America."

Hannah stood there, her mouth open.

Fiona studied her shocked face intently for any reaction.

"I'll take the envelope up to the office if you don't mind. Besides, I think I need the fresh air."

Fiona bowed, sliding the envelope across the table. Hannah snatched it from her and flew through the kitchen and across the courtyard. She looked up at the heavens for a brief moment as she walked. "This is a sign from you, merciful Mother Mary, I know it!" She took the stairs two at a time, fumbled with the key, and tore at the envelope as she walked toward the desk. She made the sign of the cross as she sat down, unfolding the page that was folded in thirds, and read the precise block letters.

Dear Hannah:

I don't know if you remember me, but I haven't stopped thinking about you all these years. I always wondered what happened to you, what would have become of us had you stayed in America, and I can hardly believe we were so close to one another yet so far away this week! I'm sure Fiona filled you in on the details of why I came and why I left so early.

I would love to hear your voice again. My business card is enclosed.

Fondly,

Dennis O'Dowd

She closed her eyes as tears slithered down her freckled face. She stared at the card in her lap for a long moment: Dennis O'Dowd, retired firefighter, now an Independent Fire Inspection Consultant.

She could see his burly frame fill the narrow doorway of her father's pub and remembered how her heart fluttered at the sight of him.

What did he look like now?

What was his marriage like?

Why did his marriage end?

What was he like as a husband?

What would that brawn feel like on top of her?

Hannah froze as she heard the door open and Fiona's footsteps at the foot of the staircase.

Fiona gently knocked on the door behind her.

Hannah took a few sharp breaths in as a feeble attempt to lighten the flush in her cheeks.

"Are you okay?" Fiona eyed her suspiciously.

"I'm grand, Hannah croaked as her eyes fluttered across the room. "I'm just overcome with emotion, I suppose. I can't believe Dennis was so close to me. Tell me, what were your impressions of him?"

"A nice guy!" Fiona enthused. "He was definitely standing by his daughter in this time of the grief. She was lovely as well. Very mannerly."

"Was he fat? Old looking?"

Fiona walked over to the desk. "Let's see if we can get us a decent picture. He just friended me on Facebook."

The computer screen lit up at her touch, and with a few clicks, she landed on his page. "There he is," she announced proudly.

The beautiful blue eyes that she swum in were obscured by mirrored sunglasses and a floppy hat that appeared to shield him from the sun as he held up a huge fish on the back of a boat in his profile picture. Hannah squinted. "Hard to get a good look at what he looks like," she said with a frown.

Fiona let a sly smile escape as she looked down at the note on the desk. "Was there any interesting read in that envelope?"

"He said he'd like to hear my voice again," Hannah replied.

"What are you going to do?"

Hannah shrugged her shoulders. "What can I do? I can't just up and leave my mother and father and shack up with a divorced Yank overseas."

Fiona shook her head. "He said he wanted to hear your voice again, not ask for your hand in marriage!"

"You know where that leads to," Hannah replied, crossing her hands over her chest.

"You're your father's daughter all right. Listen, if you don't mind me saying, I think it's a sign from God that of all places he could've stayed in Ireland, he just happened to come to the B&B that you've just begun working in. If that's not divine intervention, I don't know what is."

"I thought the same thing myself," Hannah replied, staring at her shoes as she spoke.

Fiona nodded in the direction of the phone on the desk, her eyes following a few seconds later. "Not much privacy in the house with your dad, I'd imagine. You're welcome to use the phone here. I'll leave you alone."

Fiona cautiously stood up, balancing herself on the end of the desk as a tight fist of pain formed in her abdomen. She grimaced as the perimeter of her view became fuzzy, causing her to blink.

Hannah leapt from her chair. "Missus, are you okay?"

Fiona nodded unconvincingly. "Just getting over a stomach bug, luv, I'll be grand. I'll let you get to work—or a phone call, whichever suits." With that, Fiona tottered across the room and down the stairs.

Hannah watched her tentatively until the screen in front of her sprang to life and bathed her skin in blue light. Hannah peered at the Facebook screen; there was a small box of dialogue to the lower right and a note from Dennis!

Dennis: Hi, Fiona. Thanks again for being so great and taking such good care of us while we were over there. My ex-wife's injuries were serious enough to put her in the hospital, and unfortunately, she will be facing a few months of rehab stay as she learns how to walk again and builds strength. That's a bit of a relief, as her living with me was taking its toll on all of us, and this gives everyone time to breathe. I felt like a prisoner here. Anyway, I just wanted to check in and see if you were able to give Hannah the note I sent, and, if so, what did she say?

"Oh, Jesus, oh Jesus! It's him!" Hannah screamed. She had no time to even think about the inappropriateness of using Fiona's account, nor did she understand enough about how things worked online to think it through before her fingers started to fly on the keyboard.

Hannah as Fiona: *It's good to hear from you, and I'm glad you're getting that breathing room. You're very welcome for the hospitality. Yes, I did see Hannah this morning, and she was delighted to hear from you.*

A thought bubble with three dots blinked on the screen as Denny typed back. Hannah blessed herself, tingling with excitement.

Denny: *That's great. Was there any reaction from Hannah? Do you know if she's on Facebook? I couldn't find her.*

Hannah as Fiona: *I'd say she'll contact you soon enough, and no, she's not online.*

Denny: *I wouldn't think so, based on what I hear about her father. So controlling. It makes you wonder why she'd put up with that for all of these years?*

Hannah straightened in her chair, and her face reddened with anger and embarrassment. *Why do you say that?*

Denny: *It's just what I heard from her cousin the bartender next to that funeral parlor the other night. I began asking about her around town, and everyone said the same thing about this poor spinster in a cage of her father's construction. Pretty sad. She had so much life in her when I knew her.*

She focused on the word "spinster." Hannah's nausea caused a stream of bile to gather in her esophagus. She swallowed hard. She was the talk of the town! A charity case! A freak show! What must he think of her?

Denny: *Hello? Did I lose you?*

Hannah backed away from the computer, her head in her hands. "How can I look anyone in the face ever again?" she said through sobs. She dabbed at her eyes with a handkerchief she had rolled up in the sleeve of her blouse and looked over at the main house, her eyes squinting with contempt. *I bet Fiona Burke just hired me because she felt sorry for me. Daddy's right. What an evil world we live in. Everyone can't stay out of everyone else's business.* She fumbled for her flip phone that was in her pocket and dialed her father's number. "Daddy, I don't want to be here anymore. Please come collect me."

Within minutes, she could see her dad's small white car whipping around the turns of the farm road. She descended down the stairs and out into the courtyard.

"Did that bitch in there do something to you?" Jack squawked as she flung open the car door.

"No, it's nothing like that. Let's just drive out of here," Hannah replied as she slammed the door shut.

As she got in the car, the computer screen upstairs lit up once again.

Denny: *Look at me, all judgmental. Who am I to talk? I'm living in a basement apartment with my ex-wife! Anyway, I wrote it in the note, but if you could reiterate that I haven't stopped thinking about her all these years, I'd really appreciate it. I also wouldn't mind coming back to visit if she would be open to that. I couldn't work up the courage to say that in the note, but I've got it now. Thanks!*

CHAPTER 10

CARRIAGE HOUSE 9: THE EXECUTIVES

Fiona's legs straddled the rusty railroad tracks that ran through the Ballyglunin train station, her feet kicking the high grass that jutted from the corroded rails. She shook her head at the sight of the dilapidated station and the rotted wooden posts that held up the buckled roof. She walked 100 feet toward the stone bridge and stopped at the exact spot she stood all those years ago, when she watched in disbelief as John Wayne filmed a portion of *The Quiet Man* there. He stood at the top of that bridge, resplendent in that long tweed coat and matching flat cap, flicking shillings to the little girls and boys standing on the tracks below. It was one of the happiest moments of her life when she caught one of those shillings, and despite needing the money over the years, she never spent it. A blacksmith poked a hole in the coin, and it now hung around her neck. Fiona hooked the chain of the necklace containing that coin around her finger absentmindedly as she stood there deep in thought for a moment before walking toward the office trailer that was parked at the base of the stone bridge.

She entered the trailer and nodded at her friend Philomena Furey, who was hunched over a desk. A meticulous woman with precise penmanship, she was the logical choice to be the treasurer of the The Ballyglunin Railway Historical Association.

Philomena tugged on the sleeve of her trademark pink cashmere cardigan for a small tissue she had rolled there and wiped her nose. "Keep away from me, Fiona, I've an awful cold."

"Keep that to yourself," Fiona said with a smile. "Any nibbles from the press release we sent out?"

"€350,000 today," Phil replied flatly, doing her best to contain a wide grin.

Fiona's eyes widened. "You serious?"

"I am!" Phil squealed. "Can you believe it? We were worried about the €30,000 we needed for the roof, but we got enough for ten in one day!"

"Not a moment too soon," Fiona said. "Did you see the roof since the last rain? It's a death trap! I'd love to see the comments on the donation page—where were most of the donations from?"

"Only one donation. From a place called Canton, Pennsylvania. That's in America. Have you ever heard of it?"

Fiona shook her head. She then fished for the phone in her purse, typed the town into her search engine, and looked up.

"I first heard of it this morning. Someone booked a reservation for two of my carriage houses, so I guess whoever it is plans to visit us next week. Says here it is home to dairy industries and a pharmaceutical company called Targum Pharmaceuticals. Targum just announced they're breaking ground on a new manufacturing facility outside of Galway...looks like they also made a sizable donation to the film studies program at the University of Galway as well."

"I'd say he's spreading a few Euro around town to make nice with the local neighbors," Phil said in sing-song tones. "We'll really roll out the red carpet of welcome for that amount of money!" Phil looked to the heavens as she continued. "Ah the power of prayer. After all those Rosaries, the Lord has provided."

Fiona continued to thumb through her phone. "Ah, we may not be so special after all. I remember reading in the *Tuam Times* last week that he donated to the Arts Foundation at the University of Galway as well. Does it concern you at all that he's spreading money around like this?"

"What do you mean?"

"This just seems a bit oily to me, that's all. If this is such a good thing, why not knock on the door and announce yourself instead of lining the streets with cash before you come over?"

Phil stood up. "Always looking for an angle! Maybe this is just a generous soul!"

"We'll see," Fiona whispered, biting the inside of her cheek as she looked at the ominous slope of the train station's roof.

The stones in the driveway crackled as the sleek black Range Rover made its way toward the railway station. A man in his mid-fifties with capped teeth and a complexion recently kissed by a tanning bed emerged, followed by a smaller and younger man with dark hair, a pointed nose, and a nattily tailored slim-fit blue suit. He had curly hair that was dirty blond and cascaded to the collar.

Phil hobbled over to them, greeting them warmly.

Arnie offered his hand in greeting. "I'm Arnie Blandon. We're both with Targum Pharmaceuticals. I am the head of PR, and Devan Rourke is our CEO."

Devan was lost in his own thoughts, absorbing the sights, sounds, and smells of this beloved scene. His hands traced the letters of the commemorative bronze plaque embedded in the stone wall near the iron gate of the entrance. Devan closed his eyes for a moment and took a deep breath. "Arnie, this is exactly how I thought it would look and smell. I've never been here, yet I can't shake the feeling that I've lived here before."

Phil looked into the sky. "Look at that wall of clouds up above. I'd say it'd start raining in the next ten minutes or so. Let's go inside to the trailer. I have tea on in there, and I've baked a fresh rhubarb pie!"

Devan pouted. "I thought we'd be able to get a tour of the rail station?"

"I wouldn't say we'd be able to accommodate that at the moment, on account of the roof," Phil replied. "It could come down on your head at any moment, like. I wouldn't chance it."

"That's a shame," Devan answered. "Arnie, can you take a picture of me in front of the building?"

Arnie turned to Phil and winked. "These millennial kids today; everything gets uploaded on social media nowadays. If it didn't go up on a news feed, it didn't happen!"

Phil chuckled as Arnie took pictures of his boss. They walked slowly toward the trailer, Phil's bones creaking with arthritis as a reaction to the impending moisture that was building in the air. Her prediction came true; sheets of rain came down just as they were closing the door of the trailer. Phil poured the tea and proceeded to share the many architectural blueprints that were plotting out the future upgrades planned for the site. Devan took particular interest in the archives: the grainy black and white pictures of the movie's cast and crew, the cluster of cameras and boom microphones, and the angelic round faces of the children crowding around John Wayne while he shopped in nearby Tuam.

"He gets a bit obsessed," Arnie whispered to a sympathetic Phil. "He hasn't stopped talking about the movie and this area. Did you hear we're looking to break ground on a plant near here? He wanted to be as close to this site as possible, so he's looking for a house here, too."

"That's grand," Phil chirped. "Always nice when the young ones decide to settle here. Breathes new life into the place."

Phil was peppered with questions on the history of the area for the next half hour, and the rain stopped just as they each finished a second slice of pie. Phil laughed when Arnie asked for an address to Fiona's so they could plug it into the GPS. "Jaysis, I've been there a million times before and couldn't tell you the address," she said before writing directions on the back of a napkin. "If you go past the old Crumlin school, ye've gone too far."

The Land Rover made its way through the awning of heavy branches and up toward the carriage houses. "Isn't this wonderful?" Devan gushed, looking out the window at the livestock grazing at either side of them.

"Well, it's not the Four Seasons," Arnie sniffed, eyeing the carriage houses suspiciously as he spoke. He pulled up the expansive dress slacks that were slipping beneath his bulging stomach. "The main house looks pretty good. Let's hope these hicks in the sticks have a decent Jameson waiting for us!"

Fiona waved from the window before opening the front door of the main house. "I'm Fiona. You're very welcome," she said, shaking hands with the men as they approached her.

"It's just beautiful here," Devan said as he shook hands with Fiona. "It's everything I thought it would be."

"Well, we're glad to hear that," Fiona replied. I've the breakfast ready inside. Please, come in!"

The men entered the room, which was bustling with the house staff as they readied themselves for the day's work. Arnie nodded approvingly at the vast array of expensive textures and artifacts that created the elegant yet welcoming environment that Fiona obsessively fussed with. "Your home is beautiful. Absolutely lovely," he said.

"Thanks," Fiona replied sheepishly. "I hope you like the accommodations. The carriage houses are a bit more rustic than this."

"Just how rustic?" Arnie asked.

Devan shot him a dirty look from across the table. "It's fine. It's everything I thought it would be! The movie doesn't do it justice!"

Fiona smiled. "Well, I would say not, since the movie you're referring to is in black and white! I assume based on your most generous donation to the Ballyglunin Rail Station fund that you're referring to *The Quiet Man*?"

"I am," Devan replied. He had the enthusiasm of a parakeet learning to chirp for the first time. "I saw the movie for the first time a year ago. There was a new play based on the movie at the Irish Repertory Theater in New York a few weeks ago, and I flew a private plane to see it for two performances. I can't tell you how much I've spent on memorabilia in the last week alone."

“Well, that is certainly someone with focus,” Fiona said with a chuckle. “What drew you to the film?”

“Well, I’ve always loved Maureen O’Hara. She reminds me of my mother—strong and feisty. I’d be nowhere in my life without the example of grit my mother showed me. Plus the plot and the scenery! I just felt instantly connected to it!”

“Pity you weren’t around for the filming of it,” Fiona replied coyly. “That was something.”

Devan looked at Fiona intensely. “You were alive then? You saw it?”

Fiona smiled broadly. “You’re too kind. I was around, but I was small. I don’t remember too much, although I’ll never forget the kindness of John Wayne.” She slid the coin necklace across the table and explained the necklace origins.

Devan’s eyes widened with delight. “Did you ever meet Maureen O’Hara?”

Fiona shook her head.

There was a knock on the door.

Fiona motioned for the thin old woman to come in. She gingerly arose from the table to greet her warmly. Clasping her hand, she introduced the woman to the men. “This is my good friend Maeve Walsh. She’s the President of the University of Galway, where I understand you also made a sizable donation.”

Devan nodded excitedly and shook Maeve’s frail hand.

Arnie’s body stiffened, and he exhaled slowly, proceeding over to the woman with caution. “I hope you can put that money to good use,” Arnie said with a smile. “We are so inspired by the beautiful landscape of this countryside, and we are committed to encouraging young filmmakers to tell their stories from this area.”

Maeve nodded nervously before looking over briefly at Fiona for approval. "I gathered that from the letter. It was a very generous offer, and we are positive that this money could make a significant difference. It makes it all the more painful to politely decline your offer."

"I'm afraid we'll have to politely decline your offer as well," Fiona stated as she crossed her arms. Her trained legal eye began scanning their faces in much the same way she used to do when reading a jury.

Devan reverted to the same poker face composure that Arnie assumed. Arnie cleared his throat before speaking. "Well, that's disappointing. May I ask why?"

"On principal," Fiona replied icily. "It was disappointing to read your decision to raise the price of your LifePen for treatment of anaphylaxis 600 times for no apparent reason other than greed. It's of course not our place to tell you how to price your product, but it is our place to decline the money if it's being derived from this kind of pricing."

Devan was furious, and no prodding from his right-hand man would stop him from speaking. "That's exactly what you're doing. You're trying to tell us how to run our business! The press loves to jump on this bandwagon. It's so easy to hate big pharma companies nowadays. What people don't know is how much it takes to make one blockbuster drug. For every twelve things we pursue, we're lucky to get one success! Then you have to cross your fingers and hope to God it passes through regulatory! People think that comes out of thin air, but it costs money to do all that R&D!"

"It also takes money to pay those fat dividends," Fiona countered. "I am not interested in a fight with you, but as a person who has had to rely on her share of drugs to keep alive during some tough times, I know how desperate you are to get the right drug. Thank God, I never had to worry about finding money for drugs..."

Devan cut her off. “Well, I guess you’re going to worry about money now for that roof on the train station.”

“I suppose I will,” Fiona replied. “Again, I don’t want a fight.”

“Well, that’s rich,” Arnie bellowed, losing his cool. “I’m going to get lectured by some country bumpkin about how to run a business. What have you ever run, besides this place?”

“You’d be surprised,” Fiona said with a grin. “Apart from advising the little railway project down the road, I have done legal work for the Fine Gael governing body. That had me do the most interesting work with the good people who do urban planning in Gort. I believe that’s where you were planning on doing your Irish buildout? I’m sorry to say they have some new concerns.”

“My apologies,” Arnie replied sheepishly. “I didn’t know we had a lawyer in our midst.”

“Not a bother,” Fiona said. “I get that a lot. Some men think it’s daft to imagine a woman litigating like that, but you see, unlike America, we’ve been able to elect a woman president.”

Arnie swallowed his pride. “I deserved that. If my wife was here, she’d take me out back and hang me.”

“That’s reason number 811 why I never got married,” Devan crowed. “It suddenly doesn’t seem so welcoming in these parts. That’s a shame. I’m sure others will appreciate our generosity.”

“That may be,” Fiona replied. “You better hurry up and find them. I know the good people of Gort are already beginning to lose interest in your expansion plans after I phoned them this morning and emailed the research I did.”

“You are unbelievable,” Arnie said, shaking his head. “Jesus.”

“We are not going to be held hostage by you!” Devan screamed, banging his hand on the table.”

Maeve jumped, clearly startled. "Well, this has gotten a little unpleasant for me. I'll be taking my leave."

"I'm right behind you," Devan said, standing from the table.

Fiona nodded sympathetically. "Pity you're leaving so soon. You could have the opportunity to settle this PR kerfuffle and contain the proverbial grease fire before it spreads back home. If the headlines are any indication, you've got enough bad press already."

Arnie exhaled, his eyes following the manila envelope that Fiona slid across the table. "And I suppose the opportunity to settle this is located inside that manila envelope?"

Rose smirked. "I'll leave the two of you in Fiona's most capable hands. I do hope we will see one another again soon."

"This is like two lionesses sitting next to two lambs and asking what's for dinner," Arnie groaned before turning to Devan. "We'll review the document in our room and get back to you."

Fiona watched for a moment as they walked across the courtyard before looking at the door to her right. "You can come out now, luv."

Shari opened the door, approached Fiona, and high-fived her. "My God, woman, you have balls of steel. That was flawless!"

"Not bad for an old women, eh?"

"I'd say," Shari gushed. "Amazing performance. Everything went exactly to our plan. Let's just hope they agree to the press release, and then we're off to the races!"

Targum Pharmaceuticals

For Immediate Release

November 30, 2017

Targum Pharmaceuticals is announcing "The Quiet Hand," a series of discount cards and e-coupons designed to widen access to the LifePen for poor and uninsured patients in the United States.

The LifePen is a critical medicine that provides critical and immediate relief to patients suffering from anaphylaxis.

"We acknowledge that healthcare costs are skyrocketing, and if we're honest with ourselves, we are very clear that past pricing practices have contributed to that," said Targum CEO Devan Rourke. With 'The Quiet Hand' program, we will ensure that all patients, regardless of insurance and income level, will never be without this life-saving medicine."

The Quiet Hand addresses the embarrassment that exists when a patient comes up short on the obligation of a co-pay for critical medicines. Outfitting the patient with the discount card at point-of-purchase provides much-needed peace of mind for patients and their loved ones.

As part of The Quiet Hand initiative, Targum Pharmaceuticals has made a sizable donation to restore and repair the Ballygluinin Train Station, which was home to a pivotal scene of the iconic 1952 film The Quiet Man.

"We are so grateful for the Targum Pharmaceutical partnership and applaud their contributions to make healthcare affordable to everyone," said Fiona Burke, Chief Legal Council of The Ballyglunin Railway Historical Association. "As Targum continues to invest in medicines that saves lives, we are deeply grateful for their help in saving our train station."

Targum's investment in Ireland doesn't stop with the train station restoration project; the company plans to expand their manufacturing capacity by 30,000 square meters in Gort, County Mayo, which is not far from the railway. Financial details of that expansion are still being finalized.

CHAPTER 11

THE MIGHTY FALL

Once the shovel broke ground on the new factory in Gort, the champagne had been enjoyed, and the pictures taken by the local paper, Devan Rourke and Andy Blandon returned to their black Land Rover and decided to take a spin on the new Gort to Tuam motorway. Arnie groaned as Declan popped a Saw Doctors CD into the dashboard. "Not them again," he groaned.

"Oh, come on!" Devan protested as the car filled with country rock. "They're brilliant! They're like reporters with guitars, taking every nuance of life in these parts and setting it to music. It's like Springsteen."

Arnie cut him off. "I know you're technically my boss, but seriously, dude, I've thrown people out of my car for saying less than that. You just don't say that kind of thing to a person from Jersey."

The mood was considerably lighter than their last visit when they pulled into the Ballyglunin Rail Station this time around. They could see the tops of the white tents from a distance, and now that they were at the front gate, they could smell the sausage and chips from the food trucks and the sound of furious fiddling from the local musicians. An archway of green, white, and gold balloons stood guard at the front of the main tent as they entered. They spied Phil fussing with the plastic chairs nearer to the round tables that were set up. She spotted them and waved vigorously, waddling over to give them a warm embrace.

"This wouldn't be possible without you," she said, her voice moist with emotion. The locals began filling the tent and Phil made it a point to introduce everyone to Declan and Arnie.

A woman who needed no introduction to them was Fiona Burke. She nodded to both men. "Gentlemen, it's good to see you again."

"This is the real hero of the day," Devan said to Phil. "She really had us reevaluate how we were going to market, and for that, we are grateful. I never saw a pathway to fund the research we needed, other than raising prices on our drugs. With this goodwill, our stock has risen 30 percent. It's a miracle!"

"Everything's a miracle when you inherited Daddy's money and don't really know how the world works," Arnie whispered to Fiona, who elbowed him in the ribs playfully as they laughed. "Can I see you over there for a moment?" Arnie and Fiona walked to the other end of the tent. "Devan was right about one thing: you really are the hero of the day," Arnie continued. "As you've probably gathered by now, our friend Declan is a brilliant man but a loose cannon all the same. It's a full-time job to keep him coloring inside the lines, so to speak. We could really use someone like you on our team."

"Me? I'm flattered, but why me?"

"He respects you. He listens to you. I told Devan not to raise money on the LifePen until I was blue in the face, and he ignored me. You lay out a way for him to save face and appeal to his love of *The Quiet Man* at the same time, and he thinks you walk on water now."

Fiona lowered her head and smiled. "It's so nice of you to say that, really. I do miss the old life I had at times, but I don't know how much of this life I have left—none of us do, really. I think I am on a good path that's right for me with the bed and breakfast business, and I don't really want to jump back into that rat race again. I hope you understand."

"A paid consultant—we pay only for what we need," Arnie countered, flashing his capped teeth. "Would that be a better arrangement for you?"

"You're in the right neighborhood," she replied, gripping the back of a chair for support as a dizzy spell washed over her. "Let's have lunch the next time you're over, and let's see what we can work out."

Arnie smiled. "I'd like that. Thanks again for everything. Obviously, Maureen O'Hara isn't the only fiery and determined woman to spring from this soil."

"Indeed she was not," Fiona wheezed. "Look around. The tent is crawling with them."

Arnie left to return to Devan's side. Fiona thought better of it at first, but then went to call out to Arnie for help as she began to lose focus. She slumped against the table and chairs for a brief second before falling with a dull thump in the soft grass. Phil screamed from across the tent as Fiona fell.

CHAPTER 12

THE FINAL CHAPTER

Fiona's eyes fluttered beneath her closed eyelids while the priest sketched the sign of the cross over her forehead using oil. She was aware that this was the Sacrament of the Sick, and her lips begged to move as the priest said three Hail Marys over her still body. She could hear the man's clothes rustle against the bed sheets as he turned away from her to speak with Johnny and the doctor in the corner.

"You said the children are on their way?"

Fiona's eyelids fluttered. *I hope they hurry. I don't know how much longer I can hold on.*

"They both landed earlier this morning," Johnny replied wearily. "I'm expecting my Rose in the door at any moment; she landed in Knock about an hour ago. Colin will be here a bit later; he's coming all the way from New Jersey in the States with his new wife."

There was a long silence before Johnny continued speaking. "I feel so stupid. I saw her getting thin in front of my own two eyes, and apart from saying something once, I didn't do anything to stop this. I just thought she was burning the candle at both ends."

Ah, sure, Jaysis. That's not the way I wanted to leave him! I didn't want him to worry! Johnny, you were the most fantastic, caring, attentive husband a girl could ask for!

"Aye, sure Johnny, there wasn't a bit you could have done," the doctor replied in a slightly impatient tone. "Don't let your mind go there, please. You know your wife better than anyone else. She knew what she wanted you to know, which was nothing."

Exactly. Exactly! You tell him, doc!

"I suppose," Johnny replied, his voice trailing. "It's just so sudden, like. I just can't believe it."

I knew this was going to be a shock, but it's like ripping a bandage off, isn't it? Isn't it better to have the shock and grief come all at once than to be sad for the year before and then wallow in your grief afterwards?

Colin entered the room. He nodded to the doctor briefly and then made his way over to his father. The men awkwardly embraced at first, but then when his father rested his head on his son's broad shoulders, both lost their composure. They were a tangled knot of limbs for a long moment with low sobs escaping from one of them every few seconds.

Colin was the first to break the embrace. He made his way over to his mother's bedside, bent down, and kissed Fiona on the cheek. He spotted her thumb hanging outside the sheets, grabbed her hand, balled it into a fist with his, and gently kissed her knuckles. "Ma, I don't know if you can hear me. It's Colin. I came all the way here to tell you you're going to be a grandma, and we are naming it after you. The least you could do is wake up,"

The doctor and his father laughed softly behind him.

A grandma. How I love you. You've surpassed my wildest expectations and become a kind and loving man. You're going to make an excellent father, and if there is such a thing as guardian angels, you know I'll sign up for that role!

Fiona was overcome with emotion in the privacy of her own living sarcophagus as she listened to her son cry softly at her side. The tender moment was short-lived as her daughter Rose entered the room. Fiona could hear high-pitched shrieks as she approached the bed and was confronted with the gravity of it all.

"I was just talking to her yesterday!" she screamed. "How is this happening?"

"None of us can believe it either," Johnny replied. "The doctor said the cancer came back and has been slowly spreading over the last year or so," Johnny said. "Your mother didn't want anyone to know, so she suffered in silence, apparently. Looks like she got pretty weak, and pneumonia snuck up on her."

Rose deflated the air in her cheeks. "That's my mother all right. The martyr. Typical."

"Excuse me?" Colin said, leaping to his feet.

"You heard me. This is so typical of Ma, needing to control each and every little thing so that it all goes her way. She decides to keep this to herself so that no one makes a fuss over her. Really? How big of you, Ma! You completely deny the rest of us the chance to say goodbye to you. Selfish bitch!"

"Can she hear us?" Johnny asked nervously.

Fiona heard every word. If it was hard to breathe before, the guilt that weighed so heavy on her chest further reduced her lung capacity. *What have I done? Oh my God. I have completely made a mess of dying now, haven't I? I thought I was doing the right thing and softening the blow for everyone around me, but now I've made it worse. I didn't think this through. I didn't think of all the angles.*

"That's enough," Johnny said calmly.

"I'll chalk that up to emotions running high, which is par for the course for you, by the way," Colin barked. "Don't let me ever hear you talk about Ma like that ever again!"

"There you go again, the favorite son, the perfect one, coming to her aid." Rose roared. "Dropping in and out once every other year for the weekend, and they kill the fatted calf for you every time. Jesus!"

"At least I don't have to come home every month to suck on the family tit for money! Ma put us through school and is probably funding that half million pound fancy flat you have in London on that pauper's salary you squeak by on," Colin screamed. "I think the woman demands a bit more than what you're dishing out!"

"Way to change the subject," Rose shot back. "I'm just so done with you."

"I'm done with this," Johnny said. "What's gotten into you? Where are your manners?"

"Where are your balls? Where have your balls been all these years, Da? You've been led by the nose by this woman for how long? I knew plastering you on the billboard like that was a fate worse than death, but yet you just rolled along with it."

"I did that for you, not her!" Johnny replied evenly. "As I recall, you got a nice bump up in pay and a promotion out of that deal. That was my only reason for doing that. It was my choice, not hers."

That's right. What an ungrateful bitch! We put you through the best private school systems our country had to offer, paid most of every rent check you ever were responsible for, and this is what you say about us at the water cooler at work? I thought death was supposed to be a peaceful time, but I am so feckin' mad right now I could rise up and choke you!

"Yeah? Well, that's how she operated too. Convincing you that this was your idea all along, but meanwhile, she's controlling the puppet strings the whole time! That's my whole point. We've all been strung along by this woman. I've never felt this free in all my life!"

A loud gurgle came from Fiona's mouth.

"The emotion is very raw here at the moment, but if you've anything to say to Fiona, now would be the time to do it. I'd say she only has a few minutes left," the doctor announced in gentle tones.

"Yeah, well, I'm good," Rose said.

"You'll regret this, you mark my words," Colin simmered before approaching the bedside. "Thanks for everything you've ever done for me, Ma. I wish we had more time. I wish you could see your granddaughter. I am heartbroken that I can't look you in the eye to tell you how much I love you and how much you mean to me. Say hi to Granny and Granddad for us, and we'll be seeing you soon enough."

I love you, Colin.

Johnny approached the bed, his arm around his son. "Rose was right about a few things. You did lead me around the nose all these years, and I loved every single minute of it. I don't know what I am going to do without you, my love. Know that Rose loves you so much. I know she does. That's just the shock talking. Rest easy, pet. See you soon."

Johnny's soft lips on her forehead was the last thing she felt before the fog set in, and she breathed her last.

Rose looked at her mother's lifeless body in the small coffin on the bed and frowned before looking up at the undertaker. "You did a great job with everything, Brendan, you really did. There's just a few details missing here. Do you mind?"

The short red ball of a man in the corner bowed his head. "Please. You'll know just how your mother liked to look. Be my guest."

Rose dabbed the pale pink lipstick from her mother's mouth and applied a bright red shade instead to mask the advancing paleness around her mouth. She moved her mother's thinning mane of brown hair into a tight bun and grimaced at the sight of the gray roots at the base of her scalp. She tamed the starched white collar, tucking it back within the confines of her navy pinstriped Ralph Lauren pantsuit that the undertaker had filled with cotton to mask the thinness of the corpse.

Declan Rourke inspected the bushels of flower bouquets that were sent on behalf of Targum Pharmaceuticals. Philomena Furey sighed heavily next to the lacquered coffin before leading the congregation through a decade of the Rosary with the church ladies that included both Hannah Shanley and her mother.

Phil paused at the conclusion of the prayer for a moment before continuing, "Fiona Burke was my best friend and the strongest woman I've ever known. Her kids are a credit to her and to Johnny, of course. I will miss her terribly, and I'm sure if God ever needs legal advice, Fiona will have no trouble dishing it out."

The congregation chuckled.

"Would anyone like to say any words?"

Paddy Rabbitte stood up. "I agree with Phil 100 percent," he said. "She could probably face God in a court of law and crush him with her closing argument. She was the finest legal mind I've ever encountered and an even finer friend. May God keep her and bless her family during this difficult time."

Adnan stood up. "Fiona was a woman with a bottomless heart of generosity," he said in halted English. "She was tough and fair, and she stood up to many people who questioned the wisdom of housing foreigners and so-called terrorists in her midst. I am a Muslim, but I got a new appreciation for the Catholic faith and Catholic kindness through the example of how she lived her life."

Shari, dressed head to toe in designer black, dabbed the streams of dark mascara with a white linen handkerchief. "Fiona saw the good in everyone, including me. Her life is a lesson to us all, and I will never forget her."

Rose stared at all of them and listened intently. She searched for a breakthrough from the cycle of anger and utter numbness that had consumed her since coming back home. She stood up, scarcely able to believe she was doing it even as it was happening. "My emotions are all over the place right now. A mother-daughter relationship is a complex one. I'll probably be reflecting on this one long after today, as a matter of fact. Hearing the great stories of how my mother touched your lives over the last few days as we have been going through this period of mourning will help me in my journey through understanding everything my mother was. Thank you for being with our family during this time. God bless you."

The mourners filed past the coffin as it stood on metal bars that were draped over the freshly dug grave; some held flowers, and some shoveled dirt. Rose, Colin, and Johnny were the last ones to face the coffin. They placed their hands on the wood, bowed their heads, and walked arm-in-arm toward the black limousine that waited at the bottom of the hill.

ABOUT THE AUTHOR

Mike Farragher lives in Spring Lake Heights, New Jersey, with his wife and two daughters. He is a regular contributor to *The Irish Voice* and *The Marketer Quarterly* and is the author of five books and two plays.

Made in the USA
Middletown, DE
15 February 2019